Healed

Gianna Emiko Barnes

Fulton Books
Meadville, PA

Published by Fulton Books 2022

ISBN 978-1-63985-799-9 (paperback)
ISBN 978-1-63985-800-2 (digital)

Printed in the United States of America

Prologue

It was going to be the summer to top all summers for Taryn. The worst year of her life had only increased in complications and pain within the last month. Having to face the truth about her divorce, ending up in the emergency room, finding out secrets about her friendships, and then losing one of her students to suicide, it was needless to say, Taryn needed to get away for a while. Although taking the job to teach summer courses at the University of San Francisco was a spur-of-the-moment decision back in March, it was now turning out to be a blessing in disguise. She couldn't wait for the change of scenery and pace of life that awaited her when the plane touched down in the Bay.

Looking over her shoulder, a sense of hope ignited within her that she was finally going to be happy for the first time since she could remember after finding out about her ex-husband's affair. Derek was truly a godsend for her, coming into her life at the perfect moment, to simply listen to her without judgment when she needed it the most. Not to mention, the amazing sex was better than any distraction she could have hoped for herself. He was wonderful to her, and she felt beyond lucky to have him in her life. Taryn was finally feeling happy and more like herself again. As she sat there watching the clouds pass by her window, she vowed silently to herself to hold on to that happiness at all costs.

1

Derek

It was Derek's first day back on set, and everyone was eager to see how things went. It was his very own castmates, and director, who rearranged the scheduling and encouraged him to go to Hawai'i to be with Taryn.

"So? How did it go?" Ananya asked, barging into his trailer.

"Yeah, bro, we saw the vigil, with the link you sent. Taryn is a soldier. I wouldn't have been able to do that," Jared added following in behind Ananya.

"Everything went fine." Derek gave a sly smile.

"Fine as in…it was okay and she didn't cuss you out for just showing up? Or fine as in…you two worked things out so we'll be seeing a lot more of her?" Ananya questioned.

"Fine as in we made up and we'll see what happens this summer." Derek laughed wholeheartedly.

"You hooked up, didn't you?" Ben exclaimed, excited. "You got it in with a Hawaiian chick, like in Hawai'i. That's so gnarly!"

"First off, just because she's from Hawai'i it doesn't mean she's actually Hawaiian. Taryn is Asian, remember?" Derek tried to clarify. "And second off, no, we didn't hook up." Derek could feel his cheeks flush as he laughed nervously. His castmates' eyes were drilling holes into him.

"Liar," Ananya said, laughing. "So you two are *more* than fine then! We're so happy for you, D! Just don't fuck up this time, okay? Mopey, sad Derek sucks."

"I promise, I won't. I can't afford to. And now that she's in the Bay for the summer, I think it'll be good start for the both of us." Derek smiled.

"Yo! You can make us all like aunts and uncles this summer if things go *really* well with her," Ben teased.

"Whoa! Slow down there. They've known each other for a month? Don't put too much pressure on D here, or he will end up fucking up," Jared retorted.

"Wow. Thanks, Jared. I appreciate the vote of confidence," Derek said sarcastically.

"It's just the truth. Look too far ahead, and you might jinx it. I don't want that for you because this girl seems really special," Jared reasoned.

"True. Thank you, guys." Derek smiled.

"So…where's our snacks?" Ananya joked. "We only let you go under the condition that you'd bring us back stuff."

"I totally forgot! With everything going on…" Derek cut himself off as he pulled a huge bag out from his closet and lifted it to the table. "Just kidding! I told Taryn, and she had us stop at like four different places to get specific snacks that she said you guys *had* to try. She really is something else."

"O-M-G! I love her!" Ananya exclaimed, digging into the bag. Pulling everything out and arranging it on the counter, there were different types of macadamia nuts, peanuts, crackers, cookies, candies, Chex mix, dried fruits, and even wonton chips.

"Damn! She went in!" Ben said with his eyes wide.

"Tell her thank-you for us please! The rest of the cast is going to be stoked!" Jared said.

"Will do." Derek smiled.

"Hey, you guys ready to start shooting? Everyone is pretty much done with hair and makeup," Ananya said as she got a text on her phone.

"Let's do this!" Ben exclaimed. "So we can come back here and try all these goodies."

"It's good to be back." Derek sighed as the four of them exited his trailer and headed toward set.

2

Taryn

Today, would be her first full day in San Francisco. Sienna was off with her sister, Nathan was at the office downtown, and Derek was back on set filming. In the apartment all alone, Taryn decided to venture out and explore the city. After eating some oatmeal and drinking her coffee, she ordered herself an Uber to take her down to the pier. Checking her phone as she got into the Uber, Lewis started texting her.

Good morning. Did you get back to the Bay okay? (Lewis)

Hey! Yeah, I'm here. I don't start until next week so just taking my time this week to settle in. (Taryn)

What are you doing today? I still owe you a catch-up lunch. (Lewis)

I'm in an Uber right now. Heading to the pier to walk around and maybe grab some lunch. (Taryn)

Okay, well I get off around 10 today. Would you be willing to wait for me at the pier? I can meet you there and we can have lunch. (Lewis)

10? So early you finish. You been bribing your bosses? Lol.
(Taryn)

No. Lol. I had a 12-hour shift, 10 to 10. (Lewis)

Aren't you gonna be tired? We can always hang out another day. I'm gonna be here all summer you know. Lol. (Taryn)

It's fine. I've adjusted already. I had to switch my schedule so I could make it to class on Tuesdays and Thursdays. (Lewis)

So when do you work then? (Taryn)

Thurs–Mon. 12-hour shifts, from 10 to 10. Thursdays are my long days, with school. But I have Tues/Wed off and have some time each night, before my shift starts, to have dinner with Kam. (Lewis)

Well, I'm down to wait for you if you're not going to be too tired. (Taryn)

I won't be. I'll see you in a couple of hours. (Lewis)

As the Uber pulled up in front of Boudin's Bakery at the pier on Jefferson Street, Taryn smiled a "thank you" and hopped out. The salt air hit her face with a cold whiff, but it wasn't the same as back home. The air was cold and reeked of fish. Walking by the bakery, she was in complete awe of the bread artistry. The bakers were making teddy bears, crocodiles, even a turtle with little raisins for eyes. With the smell of the fresh sourdough in the oven invading her nose, she could have stood there forever just watching them.

Turning her attention away from the floor to ceiling glass windows, she scanned the busy street. Unique little shops of all sorts were lined on either side, people crowding the sidewalks as they passed, with only a few stopping or turning into the shops. It reminded her of the Waikiki strip back home but much colder and with everyone bundled up instead of walking around in their bikinis and surf shorts.

Crossing over the street, she found herself outside a tourist attraction named "The San Francisco Dungeon." Reading the synopsis of what they were about, she laughed aloud to herself. She was definitely going to make Lewis come with her through here. He was a tough guy, but he hated haunted houses, and with this one being so eerie and having a small boat ride in it? It was the perfect setup for a laugh!

Taryn began to meander down Jefferson, toward the famous Pier 39, taking her time to look in each little shop as she passed. Excitement filled her body as she found herself in front of one of her favorite stores from back home, a body shop named "Lush." As she opened the door, the smells of bath salts and fruity soaps filled her nose. The Lush back home was a little more than an hour's drive from her house. This one? It was just short twenty-five-minute Uber ride from her apartment. And with that huge soaker tub in her bathroom now? She was definitely going to get herself into some trouble with this store so close to her this summer.

Walking over to the bath bomb area, she grabbed and packed a few of her favorites, like the Twilight bomb that soothed and relaxed you with scents of lavender and the Intergalactic bomb that created swirls of glitter and deep blue water filling your nose with the smell of fresh mint. She also grabbed herself a few bubble bars and some bath salts. Taryn was in absolute heaven. Putting her newfound treasures on the counter, she smiled at the sales associate.

"Do you have a bag?" the associate asked with a smile.

"Yes," Taryn replied, pulling out a reusable bag from her purse and handing it to the saleslady. "Sorry. I forgot."

"Not a problem, ma'am. You chose some really good stuff. Have you tried our products before?" she asked.

"I love your products! I hardly get to go to the Lush back home because we only have one on the island, and it's just so far from where I live," Taryn replied.

"Island?" the saleslady questioned with a confused look on her face.

"I'm from Hawai'i. I'm just here for the summer." Taryn smiled.

The saleslady's entire persona changed, and it was as if she became an old friend in a split second. Her tone and body language toward Taryn was suddenly warm and welcoming, beyond your typical courteousness that people in customer service often show.

"Hawai'i?" she exclaimed excitedly. "I've always wanted to go there! But it's so expensive. What's it like? Is it really as beautiful as social media and the TV make it to be?"

"It depends what island you go to and what parts. Each has its own beauty to offer, but it depends on what type of lifestyle you like. Oahu, where I'm from, is super congested, lots of tourist attractions and nightlife, lots of traffic, and you'll only find the laid-back relaxing atmosphere the farther out into the countryside you go. Whereas if you go to islands like Kauai or Hawai'i Island, it's more old-school Hawai'i. Not a lot of tall buildings, if any, and the pace is a lot slower, with most places closing at eight so they can be with their families," Taryn explained.

"That sounds so wonderful! I love that! Ugh. I need to start saving up so I can visit there one day," the sales associate groaned.

"You should. You'd love it. It's a very different atmosphere than here." Taryn smiled.

"Well, here's your things. Thank you so much and please come again. It was a pleasure meeting you...?" the sales associate asked, waiting for a response.

"Taryn," she finished for her.

"Rose." The associate smiled, nodding her head.

"Nice to meet you too, Rose. I'll see you around! Thanks again!" Taryn said as she turned to exit the store.

She giggled to herself as she thought about how Rose's persona changed the second she found out Taryn was from Hawai'i. Since she was born and raised there, being "from Hawai'i" was never really a big thing to Taryn. But she must have been wrong. It must be a really impressive thing to those who have never been to Hawai'i and are under the impression of it being this ideal vacation spot. If only they knew it was so expensive that on average you have to live at home with ten other people, in one house until your thirties, just to afford to live there at all. As she contemplated this, she began to walk toward Pier 39, getting a phone call from Lewis.

"Hey, Ti, I just finished. On my way. Where are you by?" Lewis said on a muffle.

"You're kinda echoey. Can't really hear you," Taryn replied.

"Sorry, I took my bike to work today. I'm using this new Bluetooth helmet I bought. I'm on my way now," Lewis said louder.

"Oh. Damn. Ride safe! I've just been looking at the different shops on Jefferson. I didn't realize I was in Lush for an hour!" Taryn laughed.

"An hour? Looking at soaps? You fucking weirdo," Lewis teased.

"Shut up." Taryn laughed before proceeding to tease him. "You know, that's kinda girly for you to know what Lush is, Lewie-boy."

"Hey! I have a daughter. Her mom got her hooked on those bath bomb things? I don't understand it. What happened to your typical bubble bath, right?" Lewis explained.

"Bath bombs are better," Taryn retorted with sass.

"Okay, okay. So where am I meeting you?" Lewis asked.

"I'll be by the carousel," Taryn said as she crossed the street and entered into the hustle and bustle at the heart of Pier 39, the carousel at the end immediately catching her attention.

"Sounds good. I'll see you in a few." Lewis chuckled.

"I'll be waiting," Taryn replied.

On the first floor of Pier 39, there were already so many more shops it was overwhelming. From art galleries, to knives collections and lighters, to a pet shop and a candy store that seemed to go on for miles, it was amazing. They even had a Maui Divers jewelry stand where you could open "authentic Hawaiian oysters" to find your own pearl. She laughed at this despite herself, thinking about how a tourist attraction from back home had somehow found itself way to the Bay. Taryn wanted to look at everything, but she figured she'd take it slow. She would have all summer to explore.

3

Lewis

After parking his motorcycle in the Pier 39 parking garage, he headed across the street toward the pier. Taryn told him she would be near the carousel, but he knew how she could get easily distracted and drift wayward. Adding to it all, the hustle and bustle of the pier and all those people, it would be like finding a needle in a haystack to try and locate Taryn.

Walking through the crowd, he saw the carousel up ahead. Stalling in his tracks, he smiled at himself as his eyes caught a glimpse of her. Taryn wasn't just near the carousel, she was on it! He laughed, thinking of how much of a big kid she could be sometimes and how the simplest things, like riding a carousel, could bring her so much joy. The smile grazing her lips was so genuine, with her dimple defined on her left check, that classic sparkle in her eyes as her brown waves cascaded down her back, blowing in the wind. It was truly a sight to see, and it brought back memories of spending time with her growing up. He slowly approached the carousel, waiting for her to get off.

"Having fun?" Lewis asked, approaching her from behind as she thanked the ride attendant.

"Lewie!" She smiled, embracing him in a hug. "Yes, I did have fun. How can you not have fun on a carousel?"

"True," he sighed, smiling. "You ready for lunch?"

"Yes! I'm starving," she replied, grabbing his arm.

Lewis walked her over to a place called Eagle's Café up on the second floor of the pier. It was a small place with a spacious bar in the center and floor-to-ceiling windows that overlooked San Francisco Bay. He smiled to himself as he saw Taryn's eyes light up, taking in the views as they were seated.

"This is so beautiful!" Taryn exclaimed as the waitress put menus down on their table.

"Me and some of the guys used to like coming here after work to have a drink before we switched to night shift. They have a pretty good selection of beers on tap," Lewis said, opening his menu.

"Foods! What about the foods?" Taryn questioned, pouting her lip. "You can get alcohol from anywhere, but good foods? That's what I'm really looking to find this summer."

"Their food is really good. They got some of the best fish and chips on the whole pier." He smiled.

"My favorite!" she replied, doing her happy-food dance as she skimmed over the menu.

"Other than Italian food," Lewis said with a nod.

"Duh," Taryn teased. "Even after all this time, you remember."

"Of course." He winked.

After putting their orders in with the waitress and getting their drinks, Taryn looked at Lewis, her eyes smiling. Lewis felt like he had so much to tell her but didn't know where to start. Taryn was the first to break ice, diving right in with the questions.

"So…why didn't you ever give me that letter? And if you never planned on giving it to me, why keep it?" Taryn's forwardness in her questions made Lewis choke on his beer. Her eyes never faltered, and she kept them pinned on him, waiting for her answer.

"Full transparency?" Lewis sighed on a heavy swallow. "I honestly don't know the answer to either question."

"I call bullshit," Taryn replied with sass. "No secrets, Lewis. If we're going to be friends, we need a clean slate."

Lewis sighed heavily as he took a swig of his beer, trying to drink some courage into his body so he could face her and face the truth he had buried down inside of him for ten years. He would need some liquid courage to get through lunch with this girl. Taryn had questions she wanted answers to, and by the looks of it, she was not going to back down until she got them. This was the strong, confident Taryn he knew all those years ago.

"I didn't give you that letter ten years ago because you seemed happy. I asked around about Toby, and he seemed like a better fit for you. So I thought it best to keep my mouth shut," Lewis started.

"What do you mean he was a 'better fit' for me? I just started dating him. How do you know what I actually wanted, Lew? You never even asked me, and who are you to think that it was up to you to make decisions like that for me?" Taryn leaned back in her chair, crossing her arms across her chest, flicks of anger showing in the depth of her eyes.

"Ti, my choice came from a good place. Toby? He was all put together with a solid family and career already. He could take care of you," Lewis explained. "At that point in my life, I hadn't spoken to my mom since I was ten, my family, as amazing as they are, had so many issues we were fighting through, and I didn't even know what I wanted to do with my life. I was wasting thousands of dollars going to school with no end goal. I was content at that time, partying and working, just working to get by. What could I have offered you, Ti?"

"*You*! All I would have needed was to have you in my life, Lew. *Period.* That's it! I'm so hurt right now that you thought all that superficial shit mattered to me. So what if your family wasn't perfect? No family is. And I love your family just how they are. They're amazing people. And with you? You know for a fact that I would've accepted you as is, flawed or not" Taryn argued, her chest heaving in frustration.

"Ti, your family has always been amazing. I wouldn't have dragged you into my drama, especially since I wasn't mature enough yet to deal with a real relationship. You know how scared of actual commitment I was. Only recently, within the past ten years, has my family started to get their shit together. And it was only after Kam was born that I figured myself out," Lewis defended. "You deserved better than anything I could have given to you back then, so it was just easier to keep my feelings to myself and walk away so you could be happy."

"Again… I call bullshit. Stop fucking with me, Lew. You didn't walk away for me. You walked away for yourself. *You* were too afraid to have your ego damaged if I didn't feel the same way about you, so you put yourself down and walked away before even giving me a chance," Taryn said bluntly, her eyes burning holes into his soul.

"I guess I could have been a little afraid. I mean I was scared I couldn't be this 'perfect guy' you deserved, and I was scared I would fuck up and lose you altogether if I crossed that 'friendship' line. I'd rather have you in my life as a friend than as nothing at all." Lewis sighed.

"Seriously? We crossed that 'friendship' line a long fucking time ago. You know me! I never used to just sleep around like that. Aside from that one-night stand that I had sophomore year, I only ever slept with someone I was dating for a long period of time. *You* were the only exception back then." Taryn huffed, frustrated. "Do you think I would've slept with you over and over again, gone out of my way to take care of you, and your friends, if I didn't see you as more than a friend? Do you think I would do all that if I didn't have deeper feelings for you?"

"I thought you said we were just fuck buddies?" Lewis asked, confused, remembering to how she described their situation when he was back in Hawai'i with her.

"Well, after a year of waiting to see if you felt the same way or at least be man enough to tell me there could be something between us and you still didn't… I assumed that's all I was to you." Taryn sighed, hanging her head. "So I called it like I saw it."

"I know I had a reputation of being a player type. But, Ti, I would never disrespect you like that. That first time sleeping with you, that was a just a Lewis-fuck-up moment. But if I didn't have feelings for you, I wouldn't have kept wanting to hang out or do things with just us. I wouldn't have had you sleep over after we had sex. I would've made you leave." Lewis chuckled nervously.

"Then why didn't you tell me? Even before Toby, you had so much opportunities to tell me how you felt, but you didn't. So why?" Taryn asked gently.

"I told you. I didn't feel like I was good enough for you, and I thought if I opened my mouth, it would ruin things. I wanted to stay stuck in that year with you forever, Ti," Lewis admitted on a heavy sigh. "But it looks like by keeping my mouth shut, I actually fucked things up pretty bad, huh?"

"You didn't fuck anything up," Taryn said, taking his hand across the table. "It just wasn't the right timing. I think we needed to go through all the shit we did in the last ten years to make us stronger, better people. Do you think you would be in the army with your own house and beautiful daughter, finishing college if you did open your mouth?"

"Probably not." Lewis sighed, squeezing her hand.

"Things happen for a reason, Lewis. I think there were bigger plans for us in the making than what we may have wanted ten years ago." Taryn smiled.

"True. If you didn't go through all that shit with Toby, you wouldn't be in the Bay right now to be my teacher," Lewis joked.

"Oh, geez." Taryn laughed. "But on a serious note, before we move on from this and go back to normal, why did you keep the letter after all these years?"

"I wrote it initially as a way for me to heal. You always used to tell me that..." Lewis started.

"Writing is a way to move on. You put your thoughts and feelings on paper to get it off your chest so it's not weighing you down anymore," Taryn finished for him.

"I never wrote it with the intention of giving it to you, and that's my bad because a part of me will always wonder how things would be different if I just told you how I felt," Lewis admitted. "I guess I kept the letter because it was a reminder that I did experience true love for someone at least once in my life."

"Lew," she sighed.

"Don't go getting all mushy on me. Let me explain," Lewis reasoned. "Elaine was the first girl I dated after being with you. I liked her, potentially even loved her at one point, but she wasn't you. If that makes sense? I wasn't in love with her. It was fun for the time being, a good distraction, and then boom! She was pregnant. I joined the army, went away for deployment because it was the fastest way for me to get money to provide for my daughter. But after everything we went through, what I felt for her couldn't compare to how I felt with you."

"Lewis, not all relationships are the same," Taryn said. "You and I weren't even in a relationship like that."

"Exactly! I was in an actual relationship with Elaine, and it didn't compare to what I had with you being just your friend," Lewis exclaimed. "I guess I just kept the letter for hope that one day, I would be able to find what I had with you with someone else."

On a heavy sigh, Taryn got up from her seat, walked over, and gave Lewis a huge hug from behind, resting her chin on his shoulder. "I hope you find that one day too, Lewis. Your reputation aside, you are an amazing guy that deserves the world, especially because of everything you have overcome and everything you have to offer," Taryn said, kissing him on the cheek. "Don't ever doubt yourself, okay?" she added, giving him one last squeeze before sitting back down.

"So Derek, huh?" Lewis smiled.

"Really? We just had this heavy talk about feelings and we're okay now and you're going to open this new can of worms? Already?" Taryn rolled her eyes.

"Well, I just want to know who my competition is this summer if I'm going to win you over," Lewis said with a sly smile, winking at Taryn.

"Wait, what?" Taryn sat up, confused.

"I'm just kidding." Lewis laughed. "I can't date my professor, that would be inappropriate."

"Lew!" Taryn exclaimed.

"Kidding again…maybe." He winked. "No. But seriously, is he cool? This time around, I won't hesitate to punch a guy in the face if he hurts you."

"Yes, he's cool. I'm still getting to know him," she said.

"All right. I trust your judgment for now. I have to, right? If we're going to try being friends again this summer?" Lewis asked.

"Yes." Taryn sighed. "If you promise me one thing."

"Anything." He smiled.

"You'll be 100 percent honest with me this time around? No secrets," Taryn stated.

Lewis knew she was talking about history repeating itself, and he sighed heavily. He couldn't promise to tell her if he was falling for her again because he already felt like he was! He knew, even if he promised her, he couldn't tell her, even more so now, because it would be selfish and unfair of him to expect her to accept his life especially as a single father. Especially living in the Bay, away from family and friends. He could never do that to her, expect her to uproot her life for him. Lewis knew he had to lie.

"I promise if I start catching feelings for you again, I will tell you," he said on a heavy sigh, crossing his fingers under the table.

"Good." Taryn sat back smiling at her little victory as the waitress brought their food to the table.

"Can I ask you something while we're still being open about shit?" Lewis asked apprehensively.

"Of course. What's up?" Taryn replied.

"Whoever this Derek guy is, please don't fall for him too fast," Lewis stated.

"That wasn't a question." Taryn giggled.

"That was the opener to my question, woman. Be patient." Lewis scoffed. "Are you sure you're ready to jump into something with anyone after everything you've been through the past year, let alone within the past month?"

Lewis's question made Taryn squirm in her seat. It had clearly made her uncomfortable as she fell silent, her breath becoming unsteady as her eyes stared blankly at the table searching for an answer.

"It's not like I'm saying you're 'broken' or anything, Ti. I just don't want to see you open up to someone if you're not ready to. I don't want to see you get hurt again because this time, I'm going to be in the same area code as you. And if he hurts you, nothing is going to stop me from throwing his ass off the Bay Bridge," Lewis said honestly.

"I'm not sure if I'm ready for anything if I'm being honest. But I know I have to at least try to move forward because it's better than keeping myself locked up and away from the world. Right? Even if I feel pain, at least it'll hint at the fact that I'm still alive enough to feel something. I don't want to become numb again like I was this past year, Lew. I just can't." Taryn sighed.

Lewis had nothing else to say to her. Taryn was right. Sometimes, feeling things, even the worst emotions ever, was better than being numb. It showed that you're human and you have a heart. He couldn't argue with that. On a smile, he took her hand lovingly and kissed the top of her knuckles, a silent gesture to show he understood and he'd be there for her every step for the way.

The rest of lunch was a blur of food, laughter, and smiles as everything seemed to go back to being normal between the two of them. Lewis took Taryn back to her apartment on his motorcycle, being sure to drive extra careful as she had never been on a bike before. Having her arms wrapped around his waist, holding him close was the perfect end to a long day, and it made him look forward to the weeks to come. For the first time in a long time, he felt alive again knowing he had Taryn's friendship back in his life.

4

Taryn

Taryn had spent the remainder of the afternoon planning lessons for the summer courses she would be starting next week. She had butterflies in her stomach thinking about it, a nervous type of excitement filling her whole being as she thought about how her college students would differ from her freshman back home. Regardless the group of kids that would walk through her classroom door, the one sure thing that always worked every time was transparency and complete honesty with her students. Taryn was crossing her fingers that that type of approach would work with these college kids as well.

A little past 4:00 p.m., she began to cook dinner as Nathan would be getting off work soon, be picking up Sienna, and the two of them would be on their way home within the hour. When Taryn wasn't absorbed in her work or reading books, she found an escape in cooking. All the women and men in her family knew how to cook. Their only problem was that they always cooked too much. On a typical night back home, Taryn would only be cooking for four—herself, her parents, and her grandmother. Yet she would end up making enough food to feed over ten people regardless how much she tried to portion the ingredients. They would always have leftovers and home lunch made for days at a time when she cooked.

Opening the fridge and looking at what groceries they had, she decided to make a chicken-ravioli casserole. Starting a boiling pot of water on the stove, she cut some chicken breasts into cubes, season-ing them with garlic salt, Italian seasoning, and black pepper. She began to sauté the chicken in a pan with extra virgin olive oil and a dollop of butter, tossing in a scoop of minced garlic from the bottle that Sienna always had on hand.

Once the water was boiling, she dropped the ravioli from the freezer in. Taryn then turned her attention to the cupboard where she grabbed a can of marinara sauce, pouring it into a large mixing bowl with a spoonful of brown sugar to cut the tartness of the tomatoes. When the chicken was done, she tossed it into the mixing bowl with the sauce and began stirring in a handful of grated parmesan cheese.

Setting this aside, she took the ravioli from the stove, drained it, and grabbed a large casserole dish. Taryn placed the raviolis down side by side in the dish, scooping a layer of the chicken-marinara sauce mix and then topping it with a layer of shredded mozzarella. She repeated this process two more times until all the ingredients were used. Taryn finished the casserole off with a hearty layer of moz-zarella on the top before putting it in the oven for fifteen minutes on broil, just to brown the cheese.

"Something smells good!" Nathan exclaimed as he opened the door, the smell of Italian food hitting his nostrils.

"Oooo! Taryn, what are you cooking?" Sienna asked.

"Chicken-ravioli casserole." Taryn smiled.

"Do we have garlic bread too?" Nathan asked.

"Yeah, let me go put this down in the room, and I'll come out and throw it in the oven," Sienna replied.

"Thanks." Taryn sighed. "Forgot about the bread."

"Oh my gosh! Don't even worry! You made dinner. The bread isn't anything. I can help." Sienna laughed.

Opening the oven to peek inside, Nathan shook his head. "Feeding all the homeless in San Francisco too, Taryn? You know this is way too much for just us."

"I know." She sighed with a laugh. "I can't help it though! I don't know how *not* to cook like that."

"Hey, you should tell Derek to come over for dinner! I'm sure a home-cooked meal beats eating takeout alone in his apartment after a long day on set," Sienna suggested.

"I guess I could text him. I haven't reached out all day. It's his first day back, so I figured he'd be really busy. I didn't want to seem clingy. Especially since I don't even know exactly what we are right now," Taryn said apprehensively.

"Texted him. He said he'd be by around eight. They're shooting one last scene, and he's done for the day," Nathan said, texting frantically on his phone. Both women turned and looked at him confused. "What? We're boys now. He was hanging out with us a bunch, and he did fly us to Hawai'i to be there for you, Taryn. Dinner is the least you could do for him. Even if you've already giving him your dessert."

"What the hell?" Taryn laughed. "Nate! I'm not talking with you about that!" She could feel her cheeks begin to flush red as Sienna burst out in laughter herself.

"There's nothing wrong with that," Nathan noted with a smirk. "Just let him eat his dessert in your room...locked."

"Anyways," Sienna tried to catch her breath from laughing, as the oven timer went off and she took out the casserole, "Taryn, how about you go shower and we'll finish up the garlic bread? Then we can keep the food warmed until Derek gets her for dinner."

"You guys can eat whenever everything is done. I can wait for him, it's fine." Taryn smiled. She turned to walk to her room, following Sienna's orders. "Thanks for texting him by the way, Nathan. I appreciate it."

"Anytime, you chickenshit," he replied as Taryn disappeared into her room.

As she entered her room, her phone buzzed in her pocket with a new text message. Derek's name popped up on her screen, making her smile despite herself.

Hey, my beautiful girl. (Derek)

Hey. Sorry Nathan bothered you while you're still on set. (Taryn)

I wish it were you to have bothered me. Even if I'm on set, you can text me anytime. (Derek)

Sorry. I didn't want to interrupt or get you in trouble. (Taryn)

You'd be worth the trouble. (Derek)

Don't be silly. (Taryn)

What's silly is your brother texting me, to invite me to dinner, instead of you. (Derek)

Sorry. (Taryn)

Your forgiven. You sure it's okay if I come over? I don't have to if you don't want me there. (Derek)

Of course, I want you here. Again, I just didn't text you because I don't know how this "set" thing works. I didn't want to push. (Taryn)

You could push and shove me all day, and I'd be okay with it, beautiful girl. We have one last scene to film, and then I'll be by. (Derek)

Okay. Break a leg! See you tonight. (Taryn)

Ti? (Derek)

Yes? (Taryn)

Would it be okay if I slept over? I miss you and would really like to fall asleep with you in my arms tonight. (Derek)

Sure? (Taryn)

I don't have to if you don't want me to. It's just after spending 72 hours with you, being away from you, for as long as I
have, sucks. And I had the hardest time falling asleep last night
without you. (Derek)

Don't lie. Lol. You just want to take advantage of on me. (Taryn)

Lol. Yes, Ti, I want to take advantage of you. Run my hands up
the soft skin of your naked body underneath mine all night as
I slide in and out of your wetness. (Derek)

Lol. Sounds like a good time. But I think if we have that much
fun tonight, you won't wake up to get to set tomorrow. (Taryn)

Ti. I was just kidding. I just want to be with you. We don't need
to do anything. I just want you in my arms. (Derek)

Either way, I'd enjoy your company. So I'll see you around
8ish? (Taryn)

I'll be there. Wouldn't miss it for the world. (Derek)

Xoxo. (Taryn)

Stepping out of her clothes and into the shower, the hot beads
of water quickly created a thick steam surrounding her as they hit
the cold tiles. Although she wouldn't admit it to Derek, last night
sleeping alone was the worst. Falling asleep in his arms, even having
him next to her on the plane, gave her a sense of comfort that was
unmatched and allowed her to sleep in peace for the first time since
she split from Toby.

She first noticed it, that first night, when he saved her from
sleeping on the streets after he made her fall in the shower at her
brother's party. That night, she had slept like a baby, but she thought
it was simply because the sex had exhausted her. Yet when he was
with her this weekend back in Hawai'i, her whole being felt drawn

to him, and her body fit with his perfectly in a way that immediately put her to sleep. This was not good. She couldn't start relying on Derek so soon for something as simple as falling asleep.

She felt ridiculous laughing to herself at the thought as she lathered her hair with shampoo. She worked too hard to be independent to start relying on a man now. After conditioning and scrubbing her body, she stepped out and dried herself with a towel before throwing on some cotton shorts and a university tank top. Even if she were in San Francisco and it was freezing at night compared to Hawai'i, she learned when they had come up for Nathan's graduation that she couldn't find it in herself to sleep in pajama pants or a long-sleeved shirt to sleep. She would toss and turn feeling suffocated and tangled in the fabric. As a compromise, she brought up extra blankets and simply layered her bedding. But tonight, the blankets didn't matter. She would have Derek to keep her warm. Taryn's body sighed with contentment at the thought, her eyes already feeling heavy with sleep, knowing she would be sleeping in his arms.

5

Derek

After being on set for fourteen hours, Derek was exhausted. But somehow, knowing he was going to see Taryn soon, as he drove down the empty streets of San Francisco, his body felt energized. Pulling up to the apartment, Derek found street parking, grabbed his backpack from the passenger seat, and locked the doors. The streets were quiet for a Monday night, with the low glow of the lights seemingly kissing the shadows of the tall San Francisco buildings away. He texted Taryn.

I'm outside. (Derek)

In a moment, the buzzer to the front-door lock went off, and he was free to come into the building, tracking up the flights of stairs to the third-floor apartment, where Taryn was waiting for him at the door.

"Did you stop at your apartment?" she questioned, looking down at his backpack.

"Nope, came straight from set." Derek smiled.

"Oh…so you had an overnight bag ready and with you?" Taryn stepped back sarcastically.

"I always have a bag of extra clothes," he retorted.

"Uh-huh. Sure, you do," she said, rolling her eyes.

Stepping back, she made way for Derek to come in as he kicked off his shoes in the foyer. Nathan and Sienna were already asleep, with Nathan's snoring echoing through the apartment despite their door being closed. Derek chuckled to himself.

"Yeah, sorry. Nathan is a heavy sleeper." Taryn smiled. "I promise though you can't hear it from inside of the guest room."

"Guest room?" Derek frowned. After spending the weekend with her, he automatically assumed he would be sleeping in her room, with her.

"I'm just kidding." Taryn laughed as she grabbed his backpack from him and strutted into her room.

Derek couldn't help but stare as she walked away. The thin material of her shorts hugged the curves of her behind with just a hint of her cheeks peeking from the bottom. Following her, he could feel the blood begin to rush downward, lust replacing the tiredness in his muscles. He was starving, but after not being near her for so long, his hunger could wait. Closing the door behind him, he watched Taryn plop his bag on the dresser at the entrance to the walk-in closet. He clicked the lock on the door to ensure their privacy. Walking up behind her, he snaked his arms around her waist and pulled her close, squeezing her body to his as he buried his face into her hair. The smell of berries and vanilla filled his nostrils as he held her.

"I missed you," he whispered into her ear, resting his chin on her shoulder, pushing his growing hardness against her backside.

"You just saw me yesterday," Taryn teased.

"Yesterday was too long ago," he retorted on a squeeze, placing teasing kisses across her neck.

"Oh yeah?" she replied, spinning in his arms and draping hers over his shoulders. Tiptoeing, her mouth met his, the warmth of her lips melting him from the inside out. Pulling back, she smiled. "I missed you too."

Derek dropped his hands from her waist, cupping her bottom as he lifted her up to his body. Taryn's legs instinctively opened and wrapped around his waist as she linked her hands behind the nape of his neck. Derek's mouth collided with hers hungrily as his tongue pushed past her lips that welcomed him. Pulling his face closer to hers as he held her against the dresser, Taryn smiled between kisses as hungry moans slipped between them. The sound of him alone made her wet.

"Better?" she asked sexily.

"Much better," he replied as he walked her toward the bathroom, pushing the door open with one hand while he cradled her behind with the other. He could feel her thigh muscles squeeze him with anticipation.

"Wait, what are you doing?" she teased, suddenly aware they were headed toward the shower. "I already showered, and what about dinner?"

"You showered without me?" He faked shock on a sarcastic smile.

"Yes, I did. What are you going to do about it?" Taryn replied seductively, squeezing his waist between her thighs and nibbling on his earlobe.

"I guess I'm going to have to take advantage of you," Derek joked with a wink, referring to their earlier text messages, making Taryn's breath catch.

"Well, then I guess you better call in sick tomorrow already," she said, leaning into his neck and sucking gently, sending Derek's hormones into overdrive.

"Damn you, Ti," he said, squeezing her behind as he placed her on the counter.

He leaned forward, taking her mouth ravenously, his arms wrapping around her even tighter as his shaft was suddenly wide awake and hardening. He quickly rid himself of his shirt, as did she. Their mouths not missing a beat and crashing onto each other's as soon as the material was discarded to the floor. They were both messes of desire and longing after being apart.

As the kiss intensified, Taryn reached forward, making work of his belt buckle and zipper, pushing it down as far as it could go before using her feet to shove his pants down to his knees. Derek quickly stepped out of his pants and boxers as his fingers found the elastic waistband on Taryn's shorts, yanking it downward with her panties, prompting her to shift and lift, until it was tossed to the floor as well.

His breath was already heavy as he admired this beautiful woman sitting naked and waiting before him.

"So how much did you miss me?" Taryn asked sexily as she braced her hands on the edge of the counter between her legs, being sure to spread them wide as to tease him.

"Do you want me to tell you, or do you want me to show you?" Derek replied with a sexy smile, gripping her knees and nipping at her nose playfully.

Taryn giggled as she reached out for Derek. Her hands landing at the base of his abs, tracing each cut of his muscles up to his chest before linking her fingers behind his neck and pulling him into a kiss. Her tongue pushed past his lips, and she nibbled on his bottom lip.

"Does that answer your question?" she replied, her breath heaving with her lips hovering on his, her eyes overflowing with desire.

"As you wish, beautiful," Derek said, kissing her lightly on the nose before gripping her neck with one hand and wrapping his other arm around her bottom. He pulled her off the counter, turned her around, and bent her over the sink before suddenly slamming into her with a hard thrust of his hips. Taryn let out a slight cry of pleasure on impact, followed by a satisfied moan as his length filled the deepest parts of her.

"Take me now," she panted. "Derek!" She moaned as she tightened her muscles around him, prompting life back into his body.

He leaned forward and kissed the dip in her spine before taking hold of her hips. He withdrew slowly, savoring the feel of her skin slipping down his length as he exited her. Taking a deep breath, he circled his hips deliciously, teasing her entrance as he hovered there, his length pulsing to be inside of her again. Sweat beads began forming on his chest as veins began to pop out of his arm muscles as he slammed into her again, causing her body to jerk forward on a moan. Her hands shot forward, her palms meeting the mirror to brace herself. He tried to take deep breaths to calm himself as the clenching of her muscles squeezing around him was enough to make him explode inside of her already. Once his heartbeat steadied, Derek increased his pace as he began to yank her onto him over and over again. The friction and heat of their skin caused him to groan in agony, unable to fight his release anymore.

Taryn's body tensed and quaked as her head dropped back, sexy pants escaping from her lips as she took him. Staring at her in the mirror sent him wild. Her breasts shook with each thrust, the look of her biting onto her bottom lip, her eyes clenched shut. She was on the edge of her release, and it was the sexiest thing Derek had ever seen. Increasing his pace even more, his muscles tensed as he buried himself inside of her.

"I love you, baby," Derek moaned without missing a beat, leaning his face in close as he kissed and sucked softly on the soft skin grazing her back. Her hands shooting backward, gripping his wrists, she moaned his name.

"De...rek," she panted as she clenched her eyes shut, her thighs tensing, her toes curling. "Don't...stop."

"I'm right here, baby. I'm here," Derek whispered sexily.

On a final thrust, Taryn's head fell forward, her forehead meeting the coolness of the mirror, their bodies clenching onto each other as he crumbled onto her back. His own release taking him as he filled her with his essence. Resting his body on her back, he remained in her, pumping his hips, slowly working them down from their climaxes. Their sweaty bodies melded into each other as they tried to catch their breaths.

6

Taryn

Every time with Derek was like the first time with no lack of passion, lust, and desire from either of them. If anything, each time, it got better as their bodies seemed to know each other already, understanding how to bring the other to heights of unimaginable pleasure.

"Hey, beautiful," he said as he peeled himself from her back, running a finger down the dip of her spine.

"Hey, handsome," she replied, meeting his gaze in the mirror.

"You've never called me that before." His brown eyes looked up at her, pulling himself from her warmth and turning her to face him. "You usually just say 'hey' back."

"Well," she said, turning to face him and peering over his shoulder at his naked, toned behind. "Between this face and those buns, I'd be an idiot if I couldn't recognize how handsome you are," she teased with a wink.

His body shook against hers as he began to laugh, giving her bottom a playful pinch before lifting her body up against his, her legs tucked securely around him, her wetness dripping a trail down the center of his rock-solid stomach. Her petite frame seemed almost fragile against his lean muscles. Squeezing her behind with his large palms, he smiled at her.

"Okay, sassy pants. Let's get cleaned up so we can eat food now. You worked up my appetite." Derek winked as he showered her face with kisses.

"Derek." She laughed, squirming in his arms without any luck of escaping his attack.

"Yes?" he said nonchalantly between kisses before coming nose to nose with hers.

"How about you run the tub? I'll go heat up some of the casserole, and we can eat while we soak." Taryn suggested.

"That sounds amazing." He smiled, as he peeled her from his body, placing her gently down on her feet. As she moved past him to grab a towel from the linen closest, Derek gave her bottom a little smack, making her jump. Taryn threw a shy smile over her shoulder and narrowed her eyes at him playfully as she wrapped herself up in a towel.

After heating up a large plate of the chicken-ravioli casserole, she headed back into the bathroom. Derek had cleaned up, folding his dirty clothes and putting hers in the hamper. He also wiped up the mess they made across the counter and on the floor. Needless to say, Taryn was impressed. She smiled as he sat in the tub watching, amazement spread across her face.

"I did good, huh?" he said with a wink.

"Yes, you did." She laughed, handing him the plate.

"Well, I figured one thing I know about you is you like to keep things clean and in order. I couldn't expect you to relax with the mess we made," he replied with a smile.

"Thank you. I appreciate that," she said as she tossed her towel onto the counter and stepped into the tub. The warmth of the water melted her cold feet as the bubbles engulfed her leg. Holding the plate above the water, he shifted his body so she could maneuver her body to sit between his legs. Leaning back into his chest, Taryn could feel his hard muscles against her back. Even when he was relaxed, he was still solid against her. She sighed with contentment as she dropped her head back onto his chest.

"Time to eat," he said, pulling the plate in front of her and lifting a ravioli, with the fork to her mouth. "Open."

Taryn wasn't the type of girl to enjoy being fed, but she accepted his offer willingly, her body too tired from his good fucking to lift her arms just yet. Shifting in the water, she turned around so she could face him, leaning her back against the cool porcelain on the opposite end of the tub. She lifted her legs gently so each was draped over his thighs, tucking her feet behind his waist to pull them closer together, their bottoms now inches away from touching.

"What are you doing?" Derek asked with a confused smile.

"My turn," she said, taking the plate from him, scooping up a ravioli and chicken on the fork, and offering it him. Smiling, he opened his mouth and took the bite of food gratefully. "Good?" she asked with a raised eyebrow.

The shock that spread across his face was entertaining as he began to chew, his eyes rolling in his head as his hands found her thighs and gripped them with satisfaction. "I didn't know you could cook like that! You're going to make me fat if everything you cook is that delicious." He smiled.

"Stop it. I just enjoy cooking. It's a nice escape sometimes. I'm not that good though." She laughed.

"No, Ti. This is really good," he said, taking the plate from her and taking another bite eagerly.

"Well, it would've been better fresh, but I guess one day when you're off early this summer, I'll have to cook you something else." She smiled.

"Wow. Lady in the streets, freak in the sheets, and you're good in the kitchen? I really lucked out scoring you that night." Derek winked at her, his mouth full of food. Taryn couldn't help but giggle at him as she shook her head. Food really was the way to a man's heart. "Shit, you gotta eat some too" he said, offering her a bite.

"It's okay, I cooked it. I was sampling and nibbling throughout to make sure it tasted good," Taryn said, leaning back, pushing her bottom against his.

"You sure?" Derek asked between bites.

"Positive," she said on a happy sigh. Within a few minutes, the entire plate of food was devoured as he reached over the edge of the tub and placed the plate and fork on the floor. "Do you want more?"

"I always want more," he replied seductively, sitting up and running his hands under the water, slowly dragging his fingers up her inner thighs, resting them on her hips, massaging her with little circles. Leaning forward, he kissed her, his hardness pressing up against her entrance, ready for round two.

"You're going to get side pain," Taryn said sarcastically, rolling her eyes at him, trying to keep her own desire at bay as he moved in the water so he was on his hands and knees, hovering over her.

"It'll be worth it," Derek replied, moving his hands up her tummy slowly, tracing every inch of her body, prompting a moan to escape from her lips as his palms cupped her breasts gently.

"The water is going to splash all out of the tub too," she meekly tried to reason, her breath thinning.

"Well, I guess I'll just have to go slow," he said as he continued to caress her body in all the right places, his tongue pushing past her lips as her head dropped back against the porcelain.

"How slow?" She moaned as her eyes clenched shut, trying to control her own desire as his hand moved between her legs, his finger circling her pulsing bud.

"Very...very...very slow," he whispered as he pushed a finger into her, inching its way into her depths slowly with each word. Her breath seeped from her lungs the further he pushed into her on a moan. Pulling his finger back, he slipped two in. "Does my beautiful girl want me to stop?"

Biting on her bottom lip, all Taryn could do was shake her head no as he circled his fingers inside of her, slowly pumping her breath away.

"Seeing you lose yourself to me is such a turn-on, Ti," Derek said as he began to move his other hand up and down his shaft as she gripped the edges of the tub. "You ready for me again?"

Again, all she could do was nod as he stared at her. Slowly removing his fingers, his hands gripped her waist as he sat back and guided her into a straddling position over his lap. The water around them swirled as she sunk onto him, her muscles pulling him deeper into euphoria, her head dropping back, moaning as he buried himself inside of her.

"Don't do that, Ti, or I won't be able to control myself." Derek panted as he held her in place by her hips, trying to control his breathing.

"Slow, right? Like this?" she said seductively, clenching her muscles around him as she slowly lifted herself from his lap, arching her back as her breasts rubbed against his chest. "And like this?" Her voice was raspy with lust as she slowly sank down onto him again, biting her lip.

Taryn gripped onto the muscles in his shoulders as she watched him turn into a puddle of lust beneath her. Derek was the one now rendered speechless as he began to dig his fingers into her hips, his chest heaving, trying to control his own release from breaking through. Taryn could feel him begin to swell and twitch inside of her as she repeated the torturous rise and fall of her hips, moaning his name as her muscles stretched to fit his length in her depths.

"Fuck." Derek panted. He was barely able to find any control within himself as she hovered over him. "Take all of me. I'm yours, baby."

On that, she dipped her head forward, sucking on his neck gently as she dipped her hips and squeezed again, sending his hormones into a frenzy. As she found her release, her hands moved sensually as she gripped his hair, her muscles tensing and pulsing around him as she climaxed. Feeling her release sent Derek over the edge as she blew his world to smithereens as his own release found him, and he filled her. Taking deep breaths, he tried to calm himself as his hands ran up her back, rubbing life into her body as she lay limp on his chest, her own breath heaving as their muscles continued to grip onto each other.

"You're amazing, Taryn." He panted as he kissed her forehead. "I wish we could stay like this forever."

"Same." She smiled into his chest.

Once the water around them started to turn cold, he sat up, wrapping her legs around him, her arms instinctively going to his neck as he cradled her to his body. Standing up, he held her with one arm under her bottom as he wrapped them in a towel with his free hand. Sitting her gently on her counter, he took another towel and tussled her hair, drying it as best he could before moving it across her skin, drying the beads of water from her back and between her breasts. After quickly drying himself, he wrapped her in a towel and carried her to bed. His naked body reflected in the wall mirror with perfection, the muscles in his thighs, arms, and back bulging, making her entrance tingle for him again.

"Want to get dressed?" he asked with a sly smile.

Taryn just shook her head playfully as she discarded the towel to the floor and crawled under the sheets.

"Should I get dressed?" he questioned playfully.

Again, Taryn shook her head as she patted the empty side of the bed next to her. With a smile, Derek climbed into bed, pulling her body flush against his. The feel of their bare skin touching sent a rush of lust shooting throughout Taryn's body, heating her from the inside out despite the chilly temperature outside. His legs intertwined with hers as he tucked one arm beneath the pillow while wrapping his other around her waist, holding her close to him. Before they knew it, they were both fast asleep.

7

Derek

The rest of the week was a blur. Every night after leaving the set, he found himself engulfed in Taryn. He had only stopped by his apartment twice in the last week to grab new clothes although Taryn did offer to do his laundry since she was still home. It just felt amazing to come home to a delicious home-cooked meal each night, spending time with her talking about everything and anything, and the best part? Was being able to fall asleep with her in his arms every night. Despite long nights of heated sex and getting lost in one another, he would still wake up the next morning feeling energized and rejuvenated just because he was waking up next to her.

"So another awesome night with Taryn?" Ben teased with a wink.

"Any night is awesome with her," Derek retorted.

"Well, whatever it is between you guys, don't fuck it up." Ben laughed.

"Yeah, you come to set happier, less distracted, and more energized even if I doubt you guys are sleeping at all at night, if you know what I mean," Jared added with a playful nudge.

"I'm not talking with you guys about this." Derek laughed, walking away.

"Ah! Come on, we're your boys!" Ben groaned.

Walking onto set, away from his friends, he tried to pretend as if he had no idea what they were asking of him to share. Ananya looked between the three of them, Derek before her, with Ben and Jared giggling a few yards back like little schoolgirls.

"Um, are they okay?" Ananya questioned, concerned.

"Yeah, they're just being…them." Derek sighed.

"Oh…so they're grilling you about drilling into Taryn?" Ananya asked bluntly.

"Anya!" Derek exclaimed, shook by her honesty.

"What? We've all been wondering." She sighed. "You been walking around here like a drooling lovesick puppy. You haven't come out with the cast for bonding dinners, and the second we're done shooting, you are zipping off to her place before any of us even realize you're gone."

"Well, she is a really good cook," he said honestly but not wanting to explain himself further.

"I wonder what else she 'cooks' for you." Ananya laughed. "But seriously, we're happy to see you happy. It's way better than the depressed D we had a few weeks ago. You should bring her out to dinner tonight with us. Give her a break from slaving over a stove for you."

Considering the offer, Derek began to think maybe, it wasn't such a bad idea. He pulled out his phone to text her.

Did you cook dinner yet? (Derek)

No, did you want anything specific? (Taryn)

Other than you? No. (Derek)

Haha. Very funny. Aren't you supposed to be filming? (Taryn)

Yes, but Ananya is wondering if instead of cooking dinner tonight, would you like to come out with me and the cast to eat? (Derek)

Sure. Are you sure it's okay though? (Taryn)

If Ananya invited you, it's okay. Lol. She's like the mama-boss of the entire cast. No one will argue with her. (Derek)

Are you inviting me though? If you want to spend time with your cast, I understand. I wouldn't want to intrude. I don't want you to feel forced to have me there. (Taryn)

I miss you though. Ananya and the cast just wants to get to know you too. They want to meet the girl I'm "smitten" with. (Derek)

Okay. As long as you're sure it's okay. (Taryn)

Positive. I'll have an Uber pick you up around 6. (Derek)

Sounds good. See you then. (Taryn)

"So? Is she coming?" Ananya asked, peering over his shoulder, trying to see his texts.

"Yes, she said she's down. Thank you for inviting her out with us," Derek replied gratefully.

"Of course! If you love her, then I love her! And she's a way better catch than that snake of an ex of yours. Ew!" Ananya replied with a shudder as she turned to walk into the classroom set.

Derek kept thinking of how fun tonight would be for everyone. Taryn was one who could light up a room and found a way to get along with everyone she met. He was excited to see his cast fall in love with her the way he had. Six o'clock couldn't come soon enough.

8

Taryn

After preparing dinner for Nathan and Sienna, Taryn headed off to the bathroom to shower. Excitement filled her as she thought of Derek. The butterflies of something new seeming to lift her as she floated through the motions of getting ready. They never went on their first date when she was up in the Bay for Nathan's graduation, but they had been inseparable since he flew to Hawai'i to be with her, giving her a sense of comfort with him when he was around. At the same time, despite how silly it sounded, she was nervous to go out in public on an actual date with Derek.

It was one thing for them to be intimate with one another behind closed doors. But out in public, she didn't know if she could handle whatever it was that would come with him being an "actor." She would read tabloids and see how some actors were constantly pestered by paparazzi while having every part of their life analyzed. The thought of strangers patronizing him for being with her in public gave her anxiety, and she wasn't sure she was ready to face that just yet. However, going on a group outing was different. She could blend into the backgrounds while still enjoying Derek's company in public. The thought comforted her.

As she stepped into the shower, the hot water washed away the nerves she was having as thoughts of how she wouldn't fit into an "actor's world" began to haunt her mind. But Derek accepted her for who she was, famous or not, and that was what she had to hold on to tonight. As she stepped out of the shower, she wrapped a towel around her body and began to blow-dry her hair. Unlike in Hawai'i, she could not go outside with damp hair in the cold San Francisco night, or she would definitely get sick. When it was mostly dry, she ran her flat iron through her hair to rid it of any excess water before plopping down in front of her vanity.

Derek had seen her with light makeup at Nathan's party to no makeup at all every night, and he still constantly commented on how beautiful he thought she was. Finding a perfect balance of makeup to put on her face right now would be the key as she wanted to make a good first impression with his friends but not have such heaviness on her face that Derek wouldn't recognize her. As a compromise, she decided to do a light layer of foundation and a simple natural shade on her eyelids while slightly coloring in her eyebrows. She added a dash of mascara and light eyeliner only on the top lid before dusting her cheeks with a light pink blush and finishing her lips off with some clear gloss.

Heading to her closet, she found a pair of dark-blue denim jeans that she squeezed into. Despite it fitting around her hips perfectly, it was always a tight squeeze on her thick thighs and voluptuous bottom, her cheer muscles still prominent from all the squats that they did. A simple, strappy, gray silk top flowed flawlessly over her body, accentuating her breasts but only showing the skin around her collarbone and shoulders. Unsure if they were going to be walking anywhere, she threw on a pair of gray flats with tiny silver rhinestones accents. Her black cross-body purse with her wallet, phone, and keys finished her look.

"I think I look like someone an actor would date," she questioned to herself as she gave herself a one-over in the mirror before spritzing herself with her perfume and heading out into the kitchen.

"Wow! Look at you!" Sienna exclaimed as she sat at the island. "Where are you off to tonight? Derek not coming by...again?"

"Yeah, Ti. Next time he sleeps over, can you try to be quiet? It's kinda awkward trying to sleep when I hear my older sister and her sex noises." Nathan fake-gagged as Taryn's cheeks flushed red.

"Shut up, Nate!" Sienna said playfully, reaching across to slap him. "We can't hear you, Ti. Don't believe him!"

"We can't hear her, but her face sure confirmed what we knew was probably happening." Nathan laughed.

"Anyways, thank you for dinner *again*," Sienna said, changing the subject. "One of these nights, you need to let us cook, Ti. Even if your food is always amazing, I feel bad."

"It's not a problem. I'm home anyways," Taryn replied. "Besides, enjoy it while you can. I don't know how my schedule will be when I start teaching on Tuesday."

"Deal," Nathan said, shoving food into his mouth.

"So where is he taking you on this Saturday night in the city?" Sienna seemed excited for her.

"I'm not sure honestly. Kinda getting anxiety flashbacks to the last time he had an Uber pick me up and take me to his set." Taryn shuddered, remembering the chaos that ensued when she had gone to his set and unexpectedly walked in on Derek and his ex, Lexie, kissing.

"Nothing like that is going to happen this time," Sienna said, reaching for Taryn's hand and giving it a squeeze. "He believes that he really loves you whether any of us believe it or not. And one thing we do know is that, at the very least, he truly cares for you, Taryn."

"And that's saying something coming from Sienna," Nate added, his mouth full. "She still don't like him from the last time he hurt you. So for her to defend him right now is kinda a big deal."

"Thank you, guys." Taryn sighed as she received notification on her phone that the Uber was downstairs. "Wish me luck." She smiled as she headed out the door.

*****

The Uber ride took her down the same route as the first and last time she had been to the set of Derek's Netflix series. As the car pulled up to the security shack, a cool chill shot down Taryn's back when the door opened. Taking a deep breath, she stepped out of the

Uber with a shudder as the San Francisco evening air ripped through the thin silk of her top.

"Fuck, my jacket," she said to herself as she feebly attempted to rub warmth into her arms.

"Sorry, did you forget something?" the Uber driver asked, rolling down the window.

"No, sorry. Talking to myself." She smiled. "Thank you."

The car pulled off into the night as Taryn approached the security shack, the same guard sticking his head out with a smile. The last time she saw him was when she glanced back over her shoulder as she ran away. His scowl could've made an assassin cry.

"Hey!" he exclaimed happily. "So glad to see you again!"

"Hey." Taryn smiled nervously. "I'm here for…"

"Hey, beautiful," Derek said, stepping out from the security shack behind the guard. Taryn took a step back in shock.

"Derek?" she said, confused.

"I finished my scene a little early and didn't want to risk you running again before I could see you. So I figured I'd wait with my buddy Tommy here," Derek said as he patted the large security guard on the back.

"Yes, he's been sharing those Hawaiian snacks you sent with him." Tommy's smile beamed like a little kid's on Christmas morning as he held up one of the macadamia nut candies. "Thank you! These are my favorite!"

"Anytime! If you ever need more, I can have my parents bring some up with them when they come to visit in July."

"She's amazing," Tommy said, turning to Derek and towering over him.

"I know." Derek returned the smile as he stared at Taryn in awe. "You ready, beautiful?" he added, extending a hand out to her as she graciously took it.

"Don't fuck up this time, D!" Tommy called after them as Derek walked hand in hand with Taryn toward the trailers.

The set was even bigger than she remembered now that she was walking through everything instead of zipping past on a golf cart.

When they reached the edge of the set, her grip on his hand intensified as he navigated their bodies through the trailers.

"Everyone's waiting for you." Derek smiled as he squeezed reassurance into her hand.

"Huh? Why didn't you tell me you finished shooting early? I could've been here sooner. I'm so sorry for making them all wait!" Taryn started to panic.

"I'm just kidding. We just wrapped about half an hour ago, and the girls are all fixing their faces. The guys are just chilling in my trailer devouring all the snacks," Derek said. "They're in my trailer more than their own now."

"That's not funny. I'm already anxious, and I just don't want to embarrass you or mess…" Taryn was cut short as Derek suddenly pushed her against the back of one of the trailers, smashing his mouth onto hers. She immediately went weak in the knees as she breathed him in.

"Better?" Derek asked, cupping her face.

"Better." She sighed, taking a deep breath.

"Just relax. They're all going to love you," Derek said, kissing her forehead, wrapping his arms around her, giving her a little hug.

As they circled around to the front of another trailer, Derek pushed the door open and let Taryn in. The smell of cologne filled her nose. Alternative rock music was playing softly on a speaker. Walking in, she saw four guys surrounding the table in the corner, shuffling through and eating the different snacks she had sent with Derek to set.

"Taryn!" a guy with long curly brown hair flowing from the backward black baseball cap on his head exclaimed as he stood up and pulled her into a hug. "Finally, we get to officially meet you!"

"You were our waitress at K-Elements a while back," said another with short blond hair and bulging blue eyes.

"So that's Ben hugging you and Jared," Derek said, coming up behind her, pointing to the blue-eyed guy sitting at the table. "We also have Malcom," Derek said, referencing to a dark-skinned fellow, with cornrows and a gray bomber jacket on. "And that's Justin," he finished, nodding toward the fourth guy sitting at the table, an Asian dude with a comb-over and a white long-sleeved shirt on.

"Hey, everyone." Taryn smiled shyly as Derek wrapped his arms around her waist from behind, resting his chin on her shoulder.

"Thank you for putting the pep back in his step. Without you, this guy was a grump," Malcom said, causing everyone to burst out into laughter.

"Yeah, it was like after his sister's graduation when he met you, he was happier, and then when you left, he was all depressing and hard to be around. Now that you're back in his life, he's happy again. Please don't ever leave. We can't deal with him," Justin explained on a chuckle.

Taryn could feel Derek tense behind her. She squeezed his arm around her waist for reassurance. Before Derek could retort, Ananya and the girls burst through his trailer door, their loud energy breaking the tension building from the boys ragging on Derek, causing them to sidestep out of the way.

"We're here! Is she here yet? I'm so excited to hang out with her!" Ananya said, not seeing Taryn shielded by Derek's large frame as she pushed her way to the couch, plopping down.

"Anya, she's right there," Ben said sarcastically, laughing as he pointed behind her.

"Ahhh! Taryn! You're here!" Ananya exclaimed, standing.

Within a second, Ananya had charged full force at Taryn, embracing her with a hug around the neck as she and Derek seemed to get into a tug-of-war match over Taryn's body.

"Anya, you're suffocating her," a soft-spoken Asian girl in bright-colored clothes laughed, prying Ananya's arms from Taryn's neck. "Hi, I'm Annie," she smiled, taking Taryn into a hug of her own.

"Hi, nice to meet you." Taryn smiled.

"And I'm Christine," a tall Amazonian beauty said, with lush black curls leaning down to add to the hugging.

"Hi." Taryn chuckled. "It's so nice to meet all of you. Derek speaks very highly of each of you."

"Well, he better," Ananya scoffed sarcastically. "If it weren't for us, he wouldn't have had the balls to go after you. So you're welcome."

"Thank you." Taryn smiled as she snaked her arm around Derek's waist and leaned into his chest. "I'll forever be in your debt."

"It's okay. We'll call it even as long as these Hawaiian snacks you got us keep coming," Ananya teased.

"Of course. Just let me know which ones you like, and my parents can bring more up with them when they come for Fourth of July," Taryn replied.

"Seriously?" Ben said excitedly as he shoved another chocolate covered macadamia nut cookie into his mouth.

"Seriously." Taryn smiled with a nod.

"All right, enough extortion. You guys ready to eat?" Derek said, interrupting and taking Taryn's hand.

"Starving!" Jared said, standing up. "Boys to my car! Girls to Ananya's!"

"We'll meet you guys there," Derek said, smiling as everyone piled out of his trailer. "I gotta stop at my apartment for some clothes."

"Uh-huh. Sure." Ben winked overdramatically on a laugh as everyone else headed for the parking lot.

As the door to his trailer closed, Derek pulled Taryn to him, and her body instinctively melded to his. Their lips crashed onto one another, each kiss taking the breath from her lungs as he gave a squeeze to her behind.

"Alone at last." Derek sighed. "Sorry about them."

"It's fine. They're just excited for you, that's all. It's kinda adorable," Taryn said as Derek lifted her from her feet, guiding her legs around his waist with one arm as he walked them over to his couch, sitting them down.

"Can we just skip dinner and stay here? Locked up?" Derek groaned as he leaned forward, resting his head on her breasts.

"Caught you! You can have sex after dinner! Right now, we're all starving!" Ben said loudly as he suddenly burst through the door of the trailer, pointing his finger at Taryn and Derek with a kiddish smile.

"What the fuck!" Derek exclaimed. Taryn's cheeks were blushing as she tried to hide her face in his neck, crumbling into his lap further.

"What! We didn't leave yet. We're all right outside listening. Duh!" Ben laughed.

"Sex later!" Ananya echoed from outside.

"They're right," Taryn whispered into his ear. "If we start now, we won't ever make it to dinner."

"Huh! Fine!" Derek sighed with frustration. "Let me calm down, and we'll meet you at the restaurant."

"Okey dokey pokie! Chart House on Pier 39. Ananya already made reservations. See you guys there! We'll be timing you," Ben said as he slipped out and shut the door.

"We'll be there." Taryn smiled. "Hey, what's wrong?" she said, turning her attention to Derek whose chest was heaving under her.

"Nothing." He sighed. "Is it wrong for me to not want to share you?"

Taryn smiled as her heart jumped in her chest. This tall, strong man seemingly acted like a child in front of her, not wanting to "share" his new toy. It was too adorable, and it made her melt into him further, taking his lips with hers on a gentle kiss.

"It's not wrong of you, but let's get through dinner, and I'll be yours for the rest of the night," Taryn reasoned.

"Only for the rest of the night?" Derek sighed sadly with a puppy dog eyes and a childish pout.

"Stop." She laughed as he buried his face in her chest.

"Ti? I have one more question before we go," Derek said, his demeanor suddenly serious as he sat back, resting his hands on her hips. The change in him made Taryn nervous as he looked up at her.

"Yes?" she asked cautiously.

"After everything we've been through already, in the past month together, I would say we're beyond just dating, right?" he began.

"Right?" Taryn said nervously.

"So...would it be okay if I called you my girl?" he said, dragging his eyes to hers nervously.

"Don't you already call me that with your friends?" she asked, confused.

"I do, but I meant would it be okay if I called you my girl... friend?" Derek seemed to hold his breath as he waited for her answer.

"Are you asking me to be your girlfriend?" Taryn smiled as he tried to contain his nerves even if he was a squirming mess of discomfort under her as he waited for her response.

"Yes? Only if you're okay with that," he started. "I know it might be too soon, but nothing we've done up until this point has been traditional. You had me falling in love with you within the first twenty-four hours, and..."

Pushing her mouth to his to stop his rambling, Taryn smiled through her kiss. After her divorce, she never thought she would be good enough for anyone, let alone be the person someone else wanted to call their "girlfriend." Her heart soared with happiness as he kissed her back, his body melting into hers, pulling her even closer to him.

"So can I take that as a yes?" Derek sighed with a smile.

"Yes. It's a yes," Taryn said, smothering his face with kisses as he held her, wrapping her arms around his neck, squeezing him tight.

Holding up his phone, he snapped their first photo together, displaying it proudly as his wallpaper. Taryn was his girlfriend.

9

Derek

The glow of the San Francisco streetlights had a different vibe tonight as Derek drove toward Pier 39. The lights of the Bay Bridge twinkling on the water mimicked the happiness he felt in his heart. He had taken a leap, and Taryn caught him. She was officially his girlfriend, making him the luckiest man on the planet in that moment. Squeezing her hand in his, he looked over at her, beauty oozing from every inch of her being, making his heart skip a beat as her smile beamed back at him. Deep in his heart, Derek knew she was skeptical to get involved with anyone after the year she had, but the fact that she was willing to take the leap with him, into this unknown magnetic pull toward one another, made him feel nothing but appreciation that she was willing to put her trust in him. Pulling into the parking garage at the pier, he got out quickly and ran over to her side of the car, opening the door for her and offering her a hand as she got out.

"I can still open my car door, you know?" she said with a smile.

"I know. But remember how you liked the fact that I'm a gentleman?" he teased.

"Well, in that case, thank you." She smiled.

"My lady," he said, offering his arm for her to take as she gently gripped his elbow. "You ready?"

"Are you?" Taryn retorted with a giggle.

"With you by my side, I'm ready for anything." He smiled, leaned down, and planted a gentle kiss on her cheek. "I love you," he whispered into her ear.

As they walked down toward the restaurant, the pier was packed with people, the nightlife truly transforming it into a place for adult fun. The string lights hanging over the walkways gave it a carnival feel with the neon lights from the bars and stores, luring the gazes of those who passed by them. Taryn looked up, admiring everything in awe as Derek guided her through the crowds, being sure to keep her close to him.

"Wow! That was faster than we all bet on," Jared said with a smile as they approached a private table at the rear of a fancy restaurant at the end of the pier that overlooked the Bay, aglow in lights from the bridge and boats on the water.

"Shut up." Derek laughed as he playfully punched Jared in the arm. "Taryn?" he questioned, noticing her stuck in front of one of the floor-to-ceiling windows.

"Huh?" His voice caught her attention. "Sorry, it's just so beautiful. I've never seen the Bay like this before even with all the trips I've taken to come visit Nathan at school. The lights on the water at night. It's just…wow."

The way her eyes glazed over in pure admiration of the beauty of the Bay was breathtaking, filling his heart with warmth. The simplest things giving her such joy that could never be hidden in her facial expressions.

"Thank you so much for inviting me," she said, turning to the table. "This place is special."

"Of course. We love you already." Ananya smiled.

"So did he ask you?" Annie asked excitedly.

"Huh?" Taryn was caught off guard.

"Did dummy finally ask you to be his girlfriend? Like officially?" Ananya explained.

"Yes, I did, and, yes, she said yes," Derek interjected with a smile as he draped his arm over her shoulder and kissed the side of her head.

"Yes! Finally! It took you long enough." Ben laughed.

"We been telling him to make it official, but chicken over here was scared he'd 'mess it up' or something," Malcom added teasingly.

"Well, thanks for the show of confidence, guys," Derek said, pulling Taryn's chair out for her. "Anyways, let's check out their menu."

"We come here every Saturday. Don't make like you don't know what you're ordering yet," Justin scoffed. Turning to Taryn, he let her know, "Derek gets the same thing every time."

"Why try something new when I already know what I like? It's my favorite," Derek retorted. "Don't take my word for it though, everything on the menu is delicious. We've all gotten different entrées, shared, and found our favorites."

"Okay. I think I'll try the bourbon-glazed salmon with the pureed potatoes and asparagus" Taryn smiled.

"Ugh. Vomit! You guys are totally meant to be together," Ananya joked.

"Huh?" Taryn was confused again.

"That's exactly what I order, that's why." Derek laughed, taking Taryn's hand with a squeeze, kissing her on the cheek.

"No shit?" Taryn laughed despite herself.

"I'll get us the lobster bites to share. It's my favorite appetizer here," Derek added.

"Okay. I trust you," Taryn said with a smile.

"Oooooo!" the girls teased in unison.

Derek just turned and gave them a smug look as Taryn's cheeks turned red.

After ordering, the conversations on the table continued naturally, Taryn being able to add to it here and there without feeling awkward. Derek was grateful for his castmates' acceptance and inclusion of her. Taryn seemingly got more and more comfortable with everyone as the time passed and alcohol was ingested. She was getting on perfectly with them.

"So, Taryn, you start teaching on Tuesday?" Christine asked, sipping a glass of wine.

"Yes, at USF. I'll be there Tuesdays and Thursdays. I'll be teaching the curriculum development course from ten thirty until twelve.

And the classroom management course after lunch from one until two thirty," Taryn explained.

"Do you have to do office hours too?" Annie added.

"Yes, I'll be doing my office hours the same days from eight until ten, so my day can end at two thirty." Taryn smiled.

"That's amazing. I never met a hot college professor before. I'd never miss your class if you were my teacher," Ananya exclaimed with a wink.

"Thank you... I think." Taryn smiled. Everyone at the table burst out into laughter.

The fun they were having was suddenly cut short as a tall, lanky woman, with the legs of a model and long red hair that flowed down to her waist, appeared at the entrance to the restaurant. Everyone's eyes were pulled to the door. Derek began to fidget uncomfortably in his chair as tension piled onto the table, changing everyone's demeanor as they sat there quietly.

"Who's that?" Taryn quietly asked Ananya.

"Liselle, she's the lead social promoter for our series. She's Lexie's best friend as in Derek's ex," Ananya scoffed. Whispering to the table, she asked, "What the fuck is she doing here, guys?

"Oh," Taryn said, unsure what else to say and not wanting to ask anything that would be offensive.

"Don't worry, she wasn't invited," Ananya added.

"Her and her slimeball slut of a friend are never invited," Annie, who was seemingly sweet the entire time, corrected with venom on her tone. "I don't even know how she knew we were here. She's the one that gave Lexie the pass to get on set to fuck with Derek the last time. We hate them. Manipulative bitches." Annie's body started to tense as anger filled her once gentle eyes.

"Fuck." Derek sighed as Liselle seemed to suddenly spot their table, power walking over to them.

In minutes, she was standing at the head of the table, hands on her hips, her chest heaving in anger. Her eyes were drilling holes into Derek, making Taryn's instincts to jump up and protect him from her shoot into overdrive. Derek reached over and squeezed Taryn's thigh as a silent notion to let her know it was going to be okay and that he was fine.

"What the fuck do you want, Liselle?" Ben bluntly stated.

"I need to talk to you, Derek," she said cockily, ignoring Ben.

"Well, he obviously doesn't want to talk to you," Ananya retorted, defending Derek.

"Haven't you done enough damage? Leave him alone already. He's happy," Jared added.

"Derek! I need to talk to *you*," Liselle stated harshly, refusing to budge and ignoring the hate being channeled toward her from his castmates.

"What about? I've already said everything I need to say to you and to your friend, so just fuck off," Derek said, standing up angrily.

Taryn shot up from her seat next to him, her arm wrapping around his as she rubbed comfort into his back. Her eyes narrowed at this woman who seemed to have something against Derek, making her own anger and hate toward Liselle grow despite not knowing her personally.

"You want me to fuck off? Just because your dick found another hole to crawl into?" Liselle seethed, referencing Taryn.

"You fucking..." Taryn's spunk and sass was ready to come shooting out full force, but before she could finish her sentence, his castmates rose to her defense.

"Bitch, she's got more class and heart than you and Lexie combined," Ananya retorted angrily.

Annie and Christine grabbed each of her arms as to hold her in place before she succumbed to the rampage building behind her eyes. It looked as if Ananya was ready to leap across the table and strangle Liselle.

"Derek! I Need. To. Talk. To. You." Liselle emphasized each word. "It's about Lexie."

"Go to hell. I stopped caring about her the second she left me for her boss. You can kiss my ass if you think I'm falling for that crap," Derek replied, coldness oozing from his body, making Taryn tense next to him.

"Derek…she's dead" Liselle broke down crying, her harsh demeanor falling away as she collapsed into a nearby chair.

The entire table fell silent, unsure if they heard Liselle right. Eyes were darting back and forth from one another and then between Liselle and Derek. No one knew what to say next. The entire moment seemed to be frozen in time as the horror and realization was absorbed in everyone's minds.

"You're fucking lying," Derek's voice boomed throughout the restaurant angrily as he shrugged Taryn off and charged to her like an animal. Yanking her up by her shirt collar, he gripped her firmly, her feet barely touching the ground as he shoved her back against a nearby column. The boys quickly stood up and were at his side, ready to stop him if he lost control. Taryn had never seen him this way before and it terrified her.

"Tell me you're fucking lying," Derek's voice was harsh as he emphasized every word, his eyes burning into Liselle with hatred.

"I wish I was asshole. She's dead," Liselle repeated clearly, tears streaming down her face. "Her husband found out she came to fuck you before the wedding, and he lost it on her. He beat her so badly she ended up in a coma. She passed this morning from internal bleeding."

Taryn walked over to them, pushing past the boys. Slowly, she rested her palms on his shoulders to calm him, suddenly bringing life and logic back into Derek's mind. If it weren't for Taryn's hands sliding down to the small of his back, he would have collapsed right there. Slowly, he lowered Liselle and released her as realization hit him full force. Lexie was dead, gone for good. It wasn't that he had feelings for Lexie. If anything, he hated her for what she put him through. In this moment though, he didn't know how he was supposed to react or how to feel. He stood there silent as everyone waited for his response. Taryn's voice broke the thick silence.

"Go to her," Taryn said softly. Everyone's eyes turned to her in shock. "You're going to regret it if you don't."

"Wait, where is he? Her husband?" Ananya interrupted.

"He's in jail. He turned himself in while she was in a coma. They just raised his charges from aggravated assault to manslaughter," Liselle shared solemnly.

"Derek, go to her. Say your goodbyes and get your closure," Taryn urged again softly, stepping in front of him, taking his face in her hands. Pulling him down to her, she gently kissed him on the lips as she looked into his pain-filled eyes. "It's okay."

"Are you sure?" Derek suddenly came to life again as he wrapped his arms around her waist. Taryn nodded her approval as he kissed her softly.

"Derek, go. We'll take Taryn home," Ananya said gently.

"I'll promise I'll call you as soon as I'm coming home to you, okay?" Derek whispered to Taryn, bending down and kissing her as he hugged her. "I love you."

With that, Derek followed Liselle from the restaurant and disappeared into the night.

10

Taryn

It was Tuesday morning, and Taryn was getting ready for her first day of teaching, for her summer school course at the University of San Francisco. However, the nerves she felt were not related to teaching a face-to-face college class for the first time. Her nerves were because of Derek. After he had left the restaurant with Liselle on Saturday, Taryn had not heard from Derek at all. She waited up all night to hear from him and to see if he'd show up at her apartment. But neither happened. The next day, she had even gone to his apartment to see if he was home and check if he was okay, but he wasn't there either. His neighbor, who was leaving right when she was arriving, said he hadn't seen Derek since he had come home last week to grab clothes. Taryn's mind was reeling.

Taryn couldn't pinpoint her emotions. She wasn't sure if she's worried about him or upset that he hadn't had the decency to call her, or at least text her, to let her know he was okay like he'd promised he do. It was as if he had vanished completely. This wasn't like when she disappeared on him after just forty-eight hours of knowing him. This time it was different. They had just made whatever they were official, and he had been reminding her over and over again since coming to her rescue in Hawai'i how much he loved her and would be there for her. But how was he supposed to do that when it seemed as if he was shutting her out completely? Aren't relationships more like partnerships? It was unfair of Derek to have forced his support on her, even if she had accepted it, if he wouldn't let her do the same when it seemed as if now he needed Taryn's support the most.

"Ti, you okay?" Nathan asked, knocking as he leaned on the doorway.

"Yeah, I'm fine." She sighed coldly, staring blankly ahead.

"Don't start this shit again because of him," Nathan retorted harshly, entering the room. "I don't know what the fuck is going on with him, but don't shut me out because he's disappeared like a dick."

"I'm sorry, Nate." Taryn slouched down on her couch and rested her face in her hands. "I don't know how else to hold my shit together right now. I'm supposed to be teaching about developing a curriculum in a few hours, but all I can think about is if he's okay."

"One thing you've always prided yourself on was being honest and transparent with your students. Don't change that now. It's what makes you a good teacher because it makes you real to your students. It'll be okay." Nate soothed as he rubbed his sister on the back, sitting next to her.

"Ti?" Sienna's head popped into the doorway with a knock. "Someone's here to see you."

"Derek?" Taryn asked, her eyes full of hope.

"Not quite." Lewis sighed, emerging in her doorway with a tray filled with cups of coffee. "You okay, Taryn?"

Taryn simply sighed and dropped her head back into her hands. Nathan stood up and walked over to Lewis, motioning for him to go to the kitchen.

"What happened?" Lewis asked worried, placing the cups of coffee down on the counter.

"Derek took her on a date Saturday, and his ex's best friend showed up. Dropped the bomb that his ex was murdered. Taryn thinks that Derek's been guilt-tripped into feeling responsible because the ex's husband beat her to death after finding out she was trying to still fool around with Derek," Nate summed gulping one of the coffee cups.

"What the fuck?" Lewis exclaimed softly. "So why is she a mess now then?"

"That night, she told Derek to go take care of whatever the needed to and since? He's ghosted her completely. Told her he loved her, asked her to be his girlfriend, and then fell off the face of the fucking Earth a few hours later," Nate seethed, his anger toward Derek growing.

"This is beyond fucked up. What can I do to help?" Lewis asked.

"Can you snap her out of it? Slap her or stomp on her toe or something? Anything? She can't go into her first course teaching at the university like this," Sienna suggested.

"Yeah, we both gotta get to work. You sure you got her?" Nathan asked seriously.

"Yeah, I got her. Don't worry," Lewis said confidently. "Give me your number, and I'll text you when we get to the school. I'll take care of her."

"Thank you." Nate sighed, taking Lewis's phone.

After exchanging numbers and saying their farewells to a moping Taryn, Nathan and Sienna headed out the door, leaving Lewis to deal with her. Entering the room slowly, Taryn turned her eyes to see Lewis standing there impishly, with his hands shoved down in his pockets.

"Hey." Taryn sighed heavily.

"I'm sure that whatever is going on with him, Ti, he's okay," Lewis said as he sat next to her, resting a comforting hand on her knee.

"I know. It's just what could have happened that he wouldn't tell me? And why disappear all of a sudden, you know?" Taryn's voice broke as she spoke.

"Some guys just don't know how to deal with what they're feeling, and they handle it in different ways…stupid ways," Lewis tried to reason. "I mean look at me. Instead of telling you how I felt all those years ago, I wrote it in a letter that I kept shoved in my drawer, thinking that would make those feelings go away so I could stay your friend. That obviously didn't work, right?" he joked gently.

"I guess." Taryn shook her head and looked up to the ceiling as if searching for some answers. "God, please give me strength to get through today like a normal human being." She closed her eyes and sighed as Lewis squeezed her knee, silently letting her know he'd be her strength to get her through the day if she needed him to.

"It'll be okay, Ti. I promise. I'll make sure it's okay," he told her with a smile.

"Thanks, Lew. You always know how to make me feel better. I'm so thankful to have you back in my life again." She sighed as she tucked her knees under her and leaned into his side, his arm instinctively wrapping around her shoulder, pulling her in for a hug.

"Anytime. Now get your ass ready, or I'm telling my professor you're the reason I'm late to class," Lewis teased.

"I can't scold myself for making my students late," Taryn said, rolling her eyes. Getting up, she walked over to her vanity to finish getting ready. "I didn't know you were going to stop by here this morning though. So technically, you would have been making yourself late."

"Well, I came to bribe my professor with coffee and offer her a ride. So her baby brother didn't have to drop her off to work. I figured riding in on a motorcycle would make her look like a badass so other students wouldn't dare mess with her," he retorted with a smirk.

"Well until we're on campus, I'm still just Ti. So thank you for the coffee, and I would really appreciate a ride." Taryn smiled at him softly as she brushed some brightening powder under her eyes.

"You know, I don't know why you put makeup on. You're already gorgeous, and you know the helmet is going to wipe all that off anyways, right?" Lewis noted.

"True. But I'd rather be a little smudged than bare-faced. These dark circles might scare my students," Taryn joked, spritzing herself with her perfume and grabbing her bag from the dresser. "You ready?"

"Isn't it kinda early?" Lewis said, looking to the clock that read seven forty. "I was hoping we could grab something to eat before the first class."

"Yeah, but I need to be there for office hours at eight. I'm sorry," Taryn apologized, seeing the disappointment in Lewis's eyes.

"It's fine. I'll drop you off first and then go pick up some food. We can eat in your office before class starts," Lewis compromised.

"You sure? I can just wait for lunch to eat. I usually wait like that during the regular school year," Taryn questioned.

"I'm sure. You need to eat breakfast, girl! No arguing. I'm older, remember?" Lewis retorted.

"And what does that matter?" Taryn argued back.

"It matters because it means I know best, and right now, what's best for you is to eat something. Looking at you, I doubt you've eaten much since Saturday. You're beginning to deteriorate right before my eyes. Am I wrong?" Lewis stared at Taryn, waiting for a response. When none came, he simply replied, "Exactly. You're eating breakfast whether you want to or not."

"Huh. Fine. You're so bossy," Taryn huffed.

"Well, get used to it. You'll be seeing me every morning before class, Tuesday and Thursday, with a coffee and something for you to eat, woman!" Lewis emphasized as they headed out of the apartment.

His black motorcycle was parked across the street. As they walked there, Taryn became grateful she wasn't a girly-girl and chose to wear slacks instead of a pencil skirt to school. She laughed to herself picturing how ridiculous she would look, wearing a skirt, trying to straddle the back of a motorcycle.

"Ready?" Lewis asked, handing her the spare helmet.

"Ready." She nodded, putting it on.

Lewis checked the chin strap to make sure it was fastened well in place before putting on his own. Within a few minutes, they were headed down the road, the morning chill of the San Francisco air piercing through her slacks, sending shivers up her spine. Feeling her quiver, Lewis released the bike with one hand and rubbed her arms that were wrapped tightly around his waist.

Everything will be okay, Taryn repeated to herself in her mind over and over again as Lewis continued with her in tow toward the university.

11

Derek

After the death of Lexie, the show shut down for a week to give people time to mourn. Even if she wasn't the head social promoter, her company was in charge of a lot of marketing for Netflix, with Lexie taking lead on most of the projects. So all production of their shows shut down as a sign of respect for her. Derek had gone with her best friend, Liselle, to the hospital down in San Jose that Saturday night to pay respects to the family and say a final farewell to Lexie.

Instead of getting the cold greeting he expected, her family embraced him and kept noting how Lexie would still be alive if she had stayed with Derek. They kept saying how much they loved him and how they always considered him as part of the family. Her mom even asked why Derek never proposed to her. Little did her mom know that her *little angel* was the one who didn't want to be with him.

Seeing Lexie's frail body in the hospital bed made his knees almost give out under him. He had to grip the bed rails to steady himself. Her typically tan skin looked ghostly and pale. Her once vibrant gold locks were now dull against the fluorescent hospital lights. Bruises showered her face and arms, her lips were broken and cut with some dried blood still matted on her skin. The monitor in the room was the only sound he could remember as tubes seemed to go in and out of her everywhere. His heart ached for her, thinking of how afraid and alone she must have felt in those last moments.

Derek didn't realize how much he still cared for her until he saw her there lifeless in the hospital bed. She was his first love and would always hold a special place in his heart. But the fact that he let his anger and hurt cloud his judgement, blinding him from her cries for help, he felt ashamed. He somehow felt responsible for her death as if not listening to her, not digging deeper into why she was suddenly running to him, was his fault. How could he say that she was his first love and that he cared for her if he couldn't save her? If he pushed her away when she reached out and needed him the most?

Needing to escape from everything for a little while, he took the first flight down to LA after leaving the hospital. He immediately headed to his childhood home, tucked away in the Sherman Oaks hillsides. His parents were in shock when he rang the doorbell early Sunday morning, quick to embrace him when they saw the apparent distress written across his face. They gave him the afternoon to himself, and he remained locked inside of his room, his mind blank and his body numb to everything else around him, home only giving him a slight sense of comfort. Monday went the same for Derek as well, with him only leaving his room to use the restroom and refill his glass of whiskey. Besides trying to drink the guilt away, Derek sat on his bed, staring at the walls as if they held the answers on how to move on. By Tuesday, without any sleep, he was practically a zombie waiting for the darkness closing in around him to finally take him so he could rest, so he could finally have peace.

"D?" A soft voice drifted under his door, but it wasn't the voice of his mother. "It's Emma. Mom told me you were home. Can you please open up?"

"I don't want to talk to anyone right now, Em, I'm sorry," he said to the door.

"Really? You're going to keep your baby sister who drove all the way here locked out?" Emma whined.

"Yes," Derek said shortly.

"Really? Really though?" Emma said, the pouting of her lower lip clear in her tone even if he couldn't see it.

"Huh! You're such a pain!" Derek grumbled, climbing off his bed and unlocking his door. As he started at his little sister standing before him with a smile, he sighed. "You can't use the 'baby sis' card forever, you know? You are an adult now."

"I know, but no matter how old we get, I'll always be your baby sis." Emma smiled, holding her arms out for a hug that Derek happily embraced. "Ew, you smell. When was the last time you showered?"

"Saturday morning." Derek laughed, squeezing Emma's face into his armpit as she made gagging sounds.

"Stop! You're going to kill me with your stench, you nasty!" She laughed as she pushed him away. After calming down and giving her brother the one-over, she sighed heavily. "On a serious note though, D, what the fuck is going on? What happened?"

Sighing heavily, Derek turned and slumped at the foot of his bed, his sister taking the same position opposite of him against his wall. Derek's heart felt like it was being pulled in a million directions, and he had no idea where to start.

"Lexie died. She's the marketing executive they've been talking about on the news that was beaten to death. Her family and company have been keeping the details under wraps to salvage reputations or whatever, especially since it's still an open investigation and her boss/ husband is their prime suspect right now," Derek summed.

"Whoa. Okay, wasn't expecting that." Emma sighed with wide eyes. "I'm sorry about Lexie. I know she hurt you, and I don't particularly care for the girl, but no one deserves to die like that."

"Exactly." Derek sighed. "I just don't know how I'm supposed to feel about it all, you know? And I feel really dumb talking about it to my little sister."

"Well, pretend I'm not here then. Just vent. It doesn't have to make sense, but sometimes, you just need to talk about your shit to sort through it," Emma replied.

Derek sighed heavily as he dropped his head backward, resting it on his bed. "I feel angry. I'm mad at her for not staying with me. I'm mad at her husband for being a dick and killing her. I'm mad at myself for not knowing she was in trouble so I could protect her. And this guilt that I feel for hating her so much that I didn't give myself a chance to talk to her one last time. It's all just…"

"Derek, you couldn't have protected her from herself. It was her choice that resulted in her being in that relationship. Just like you can't protect me like that anymore. I'm an adult, and I need to face the consequences of my own actions. You're awesome, D, but you can't protect everyone, and you can't beat yourself up for everyone else's fuckups," Emma interrupted.

"I know." Derek sighed. "But still, it's just…too much."

"And even if she were alive, would you even want to talk to her? Whether you were mad at her or not, would you want to talk to her after everything she put you though?" Emma tried to reason.

"Yes…no… I don't know. It just bothers me that the last conversation we had was me having her escorted and banned from my set," Derek said with guilt.

"As you should have because she broke onto your set! You were happy for her, gave her your well wishes when you found out she was engaged, within a few weeks of you two breaking up at that, *and* you always tried to be the bigger person. *She* kept pushing it. *She* was the one who wanted her cake and to eat it too. That's not your fault, D!" Emma seethed.

"Yeah, but the fact that the last thing I ever said to her was cold, I just feel messed up about it. Like I should've said something else." Derek hung his head.

"Like what? What else were you supposed to say to that?" Emma scoffed.

"I don't know. I just feel shitty about it, okay?" Derek sighed.

"You know what you should feel shitty about? Ghosting Taryn! Nathan called me this morning, you jackass!" Emma fired at her brother, realizing his guilt was pushing away the best thing that had ever happened to him.

Upon hearing her name, it was as if a shot of life was injected into his body and he was sitting up, suddenly snapped back to reality. *Taryn.* He hadn't talked to her since the restaurant on Saturday. Fuck! Now anxiety and guilt were filling his body for different reasons. He was so used to being alone at this point he didn't know how to consider someone else before he did things.

"Is she okay?" Derek finally asked.

"Is she okay? Would you be okay if she asked you to be her boyfriend, told you she loved you, and then disappeared on you altogether?" Emma barked at him.

"She disappeared on me before!" he retorted.

"This is *not* the same thing, Derek, and you know it! You guys were barely anything, a one-night stand at the most, and she saw you with Lexie. That's why she disappeared from you, and even then, she at least had the decency to write you the letter! You didn't even tell her you were coming home!" Emma argued, standing up, lecturing Derek like he was the younger sibling. "On top of that, do you know how stir-crazy she must be right now when you *promised* her you were going to call and go to home to her? But then just leave without so much as a text to let her know where you are or that you're okay so she's not worried?"

"I'm sorry, okay? I wasn't thinking! Maybe, Taryn is better off without me. Maybe, it's better if she doesn't hear from me again. I'm too damaged. I don't even know what I feel anymore." He shrugged with self-pity.

"I want to punch you in the face right now, you idiot! You're never thinking. You weren't thinking when you kissed Lexie. You weren't thinking when you flew to Hawai'i for Taryn. You weren't thinking when you came home without a word! But don't you dare try and turn this around and make like *you're* the victim here. Yeah, you're hurting, Derek. I get it, but don't push away the best thing to ever walk into your life right now because you want to have a pity party for yourself over a girl who never even cared about you!" Emma yelled, fists clenched.

Derek wouldn't admit it, but she was absolutely right about everything right now, so he just sat there and took the lecture. His gaze dropped to the floor as his sister's rampage continued full force.

"And don't pull this 'I'm damaged' crap! If anything, Taryn is the one who is beyond damaged. With everything she's been through, *she* of all people has the right to curl up under a rock and want to hide from the world. Yet you don't see her doing that, do you? No, she's not! She's out there, still trying to help others, still trying to move forward with her life, and still caring about you! If you owe anyone an apology right now, it's Taryn. So stop being this crybaby bitch and man up, Derek!" Emma sighed frustratedly, storming out of his room, slamming the door behind her.

Derek knew he was in the wrong, but to ask Taryn for yet another chance when he's already hurt her before was ludicrous. Even he knew that she thinks it would be dumb on her part to give him another chance. How could he ever make it okay between them after what he put her through this weekend? He wasn't ready to go back to the Bay and face her or Nathan. If this was the wrath he got from his sister, he was beyond nervous to see what choice words Nathan would have saved up for him. Even after she was out of his life, Lexie still had this invisible hold on him, but he couldn't let that rule his judgments anymore. He had to follow his heart with Taryn and find a way to move forward.

12

Lewis

Sitting in the lounge after the first class, Taryn seemed rejuvenated. She had ordered them french-dip sandwiches, with crisscut fries and strawberry milkshakes from Mel's Diner. Lewis met the UberEATS delivery guy and headed to meet Taryn for lunch. He was happy to see that she was doing better than the mess she was in the morning. Even if he had gotten her coffee and oatmeal from McDonald's, she barely touched it. So he was glad she was making an effort to at least eat something, anything before she passed out on him.

"Feeling better?" Lewis asked as she smiled, taking a swig of her milkshake.

"Much." She nodded. "Being in front of a class, getting to know your students, it's my happy place. I think I needed to be teaching today. It helped me feel better."

"Well, you did awesome. I would never know that outside of that class, you're this dorky, clumsy, weird person," Lewis teased as he bit into a french fry.

"Uh!" Taryn scoffed before breaking out into a laugh and sighing. "I guess. Those three words do sum up my personality once you get to know me."

"Yeah, but in front of the class, it was like watching a totally different person! You exuded confidence, and you have this strong presence that demands attention, *and* you can tell you have a passion for what you do. It's admirable. Everyone was whispering about how badass you were in class," Lewis explained.

"What?" Taryn asked, confused.

"Everyone was talking about how great of a professor you were. The girl sitting next to me said she hopes she can be like you when she's in front of her own classroom," Lewis admitted.

"Shut up, they weren't saying that. You're just trying to boost my confidence because I sucked. I was so nervous." Taryn blushed.

"I'm serious! You're a badass when it comes to teaching. Don't doubt yourself. It was seriously intimidating being on the receiving end of your lecture." Lewis laughed. "And I promise, I only heard positive comments about you. I was listening very intently because if anyone were to talk shit, they would've got their ass whopped."

"Well, thanks. I appreciate it." Taryn smiled. "One more class to go. This one should be fun. Classroom management is my jam."

"I'm excited for it then. Although I'm not sure how they turned that into an entire class of its own. Isn't classroom management just keeping the class in line so you can teach?" Lewis asked, confused.

"That's just part of it. Classroom management embodies relationship building, creating a positive and safe learning environment, effective student collaboration, and just knowing what your kids need so you can provide proper supports to help them be successful. Without all of that, you can't manage your class, and it becomes very difficult to get kids to want to learn from you," Taryn explained.

"Damn, well. It's a good thing I'm taking that class then. Looking forward to learning from the best." He winked.

"Shut up and eat." Taryn laughed.

As they finished their lunch, they spoke lightly about San Francisco. Lewis talked about his daughter with a pride that made Taryn's heart melt. In turn, Taryn told him about how different teaching college students was from her freshman back home. All the while, Lewis made a conscious effort to avoid all conversation and topics that could leave her mind trailing to thoughts of Derek. He didn't want her to fall into a funk before her next class.

After lunch, they walked over to the bookstore to browse the university merchandise. Lewis made a game out of trying on the girls' clothing in an attempt to get Taryn laughing. In the corner of the store, a beautiful green, yellow, and tan hand-knit blanket caught her eye. It had the University of San Francisco emblem on it and was so soft to the touch it could comfort anyone after a long day. Taryn grabbed it and headed toward the register, handing it to the store clerk. As a show of appreciation, Lewis threw cash down before she could pay.

"What are you doing?" Taryn scoffed, as she froze with her credit card in her hand.

"Paying. You know this green paper? You trade it in exchange for different items in this city," Lewis teased.

"Wise ass. I know that, but why are you paying? I can buy my own shit," Taryn argued.

"I know you can, my independent, stubborn friend, but for once in your life, can you please let someone do something nice for you? For no reason? Just to see you smile?" Lewis retorted.

"Huh. You're annoying, you know that?" Taryn said on a huff as Lewis yanked her credit card from her hand and shoved it back into her bag.

"I know, but it's a cute kinda annoying, right?" He smiled.

"Hmmm…not sure about *that*." Taryn laughed.

"Damn, I gotta step up my cuteness then," Lewis joked as he took the blanket from the clerk and gave it to Taryn. "Here you go, spoiled girl."

"Hey! I could've…" Taryn started to argue.

"I'm kidding," Lewis interrupted with a laugh. "Geez, you, college professors, are so sensitive!"

The two of them began walking to the next class up on Lone Mountain as Taryn stared up at the campus buildings. The architecture alone was to die for. To this day, she couldn't get over the beauty of the campus chapel where the graduation took place. The amazement, clear on her face, made Lewis smile to himself as they walked. Yep, Taryn was something else.

As they entered the classroom, students slowly started to trickle in. Lewis sat at the back of the class as a way to give her space. He didn't want her to feel like he was analyzing her every move by sitting front and center. Promptly at 1:00 p.m., Taryn started class and pro-jected the faces of six students on the board.

"Good afternoon, class. My name is Taryn, you can call me Ms. Ti," she began.

"Um, you don't want us to call you professor or anything?" a female student in a yellow sweatshirt asked meekly from the second row. It was the same question someone in the first course asked when she introduced herself.

"No." Taryn smiled gently. "Although I do have my MEd and my EdD, I don't like titles. Too intimidating."

"Oh, okay. Thank you, Ms. Ti." The girl sighed, surprised.

"What is your name?" Taryn asked the girl in yellow.

"Sylvia," she said meekly.

"Well, it is nice to meet you, Sylvia. Is there a nickname you go by that you'd prefer I call you?" Taryn continued.

"Vee," the girl replied cautiously.

"Well, Vee, it is very nice to meet you." Taryn smiled at Sylvia warmly. Turning to the rest of the class, she stated, "There was lesson number 1 in classroom management. The one thing you need to take away from this class is the importance of getting to know your students. They are not just 'kids' who come and go. Each of them has a story, and if you take the time to get to know their stories, they'll take the time to listen to what you have to teach them."

The whole class nodded in amazement. Taryn was killing it. This really was her forte. Walking up to the board with her laser pointer, she continued.

"Like I said, every kid has a story. Some worse than others, some going through things that, as an adult, I would not even be able to deal with. But this is the reality for many kids. These six faces are my own students from back home, six of my former freshmen who had the biggest impact on me and my journey as an educator," she said, pointing to each of the kids projected on her board. "Each week, for the first six weeks of this course, I will share with you one of their stories. We will discuss different management strategies to use to sup-port their needs, and based on strategies you've come up with, we'll see at the end of the week which of those strategies were successful in helping them to learn your classroom."

"So we're going to be graded on whether or not the strategies work? How do we know if we're doing this all hypothetically?" Sylvia asked.

"You'll know because the strategies I'm going to introduce each week are the very ones I've tried with these kids. And, no, you will not be graded on how well the strategy works. Instead, you will be graded on how well you can adapt and accommodate these strategies to meet the individual needs that you identify based on hearing their stories," Taryn replied. "Hint, I just gave you guys the key to passing this class." She winked as she turned and grabbed a stack of papers from her desk.

Everyone opened their notebooks and laptops and began noting the "hint" that she gave to them. Damn, if Lewis had a teacher like her in high school, maybe he would have wanted to get into education that much sooner. As she passed out the course syllabus, everyone began flipping through it to review the breakdown of the course, the expectations, and the grading scale.

"Ms. Ti?" Sylvia asked, raising her hand. "What is this 'mock' classroom project in the last two weeks? It says it's 50 percent of our overall grade."

"Great question! In the 'mock' classroom project, I will become part of the class, as a student, embodying a specific challenge or background story. You will partner with a peer to 'teach' the classroom, and you will need to implement the strategies you learned to help me be successful in your class." Taryn smiled.

"So we get to actually try the strategies?" Sylvia asked.

"Yes, Vee, you get to try them out. I'm more of a visual, kinesthetic learner, so this class won't be one where I only have you guys do bookwork. I would get bored myself." Taryn laughed as the rest of the class let out a chuckle.

Lewis looked around at all his classmates, completely taken by Taryn already, and they were only forty-five minutes into class!

"Okay, I want you guys to review the syllabus at home, come on Thursday with any other questions you may have *before* you sign it. Don't sign anything you're not sure of, yeah?" Taryn started. "Homework tonight, you need to go onto the university portal for our class. Watch the video on my first student, read his background story, and take some notes on the difficulties he faced in his life to prep for our strategy examination on Thursday. Everyone got that?"

"Yes," the class said in unison, nodding their understanding.

"Now, let's get to know each other!" She smiled as she jumped up on the teacher desk at the front of the class and crossed her legs under her. Taryn switched to the next slide on the projector where five questions appeared. "We're going to go around and take turns answering the five questions projected behind me. Let's get started!"

1. What is your name and/or nickname?
2. What do you think classroom management is?
3. Describe a teacher in your past who you considered as having "good" classroom management.
4. Why did you want to go into teaching?
5. What are your hobbies outside of school?

After answering the questions herself, she proceeded to go around the class, giving each student a chance to answer the questions. Shockingly, everyone's answers to question number 2 were different.

"Ms. Ti? Why is it that we all have different views of what classroom management is?" a young man in a gray sweater vest, named Tanner, asked after everyone had shared.

"It's because everyone's classroom management is different based on your different experiences. You have to find your own style, and what works for you might not work for someone else. These strategies that I'll be teaching you will help you to find your style, and your ability to adapt it to different types of students you may encounter in the classroom will be the goal for you to achieve by the end of this course," Taryn explained.

"So did you get to know us through those questions, Ms. Ti?" Sylvia asked.

"Yes, I did, Vee, but just because I know your name and got a brief insight into how you think, it doesn't mean I know you on the level that I need to in order to be an effective teacher for you. Getting to know you guys is a process, a condensed one for the summer but a process nonetheless, especially when you're in your own class. Some kids will open up from day one, while others may need time to be convinced that you actually care about them before they open up to you. It's an ongoing, continuous process." Taryn smiled, looking down at her phone. "Well, that's all the time we have for today, class. Don't forget your homework, and remember to review the syllabus. Have a great day!"

"You too, Ms. Ti!" Sylvia said, giving her a high five.

"You did awesome, Ms. Ti." Lewis smirked as he got up from his desk and walked to the front of the class after everyone had left. "I'm really impressed to be honest."

"Thanks, Lewie. It means a lot coming from you. Could you tell I was nervous?" she asked after the last student left.

"No, you were as cool as a cucumber." He smiled.

"Excuse me. Sorry to interrupt. I have a delivery for Taryn Okata?" a delivery man said as he peeked his head into the classroom.

"I'm Taryn," she said apprehensively.

"Here you go, ma'am," the delivery man said as he entered the class with a huge vase filled with two dozen red roses and a card sitting atop them on a stick.

"Thank you," Taryn said to him, taking the flowers and placing them down on her desk as the delivery man left.

"Who are they from?" Lewis asked.

Opening the card, Taryn's body became rigid as the air in the room seemed to be vacuumed out. She froze, staring down at the simple phrase written on the card before her eyes hovered over the sender's name. She swallowed hard, trying to suppress the tears that suddenly threatened to break free. The card read,

I'm sorry.

—*Derek*

Lewis didn't know what to do, but after what seemed like ages that they were just standing there, both of them frozen in time, he bent down a little to look at her face. Her eyes were glazed over but empty. Her facial expression was completely blank, and it seemed as if she were holding her breath.

"Ti?" he said gently, placing his hand on her forearm, his worry for his friend growing with each second that passed.

Without saying anything, Taryn snapped. She dropped the card, picked up the vase, and slammed it to the floor with a ferocity that he had never seen from her before, making Lewis jump back in shock. He had no idea what the hell just happened, but she suddenly crumbled to the floor, her knees resting on the shards of glass as she dropped her face to her hands and tears began to pour freely from her eyes. Her sobs were echoing in the empty classroom.

"Ti!" he exclaimed, rushing over to her and squatting next to her quaking body. "Are you okay?"

"No," she sobbed honestly. "I finally open up again to someone and am under the impression he feels the same. Only for him to ghost me after he tells me he supposedly loves me? And all he has to say to me after three fucking days is that he's sorry? Not even having the decency to text me or call me to say it? He sends flowers and says it in a fucking card? Like that is supposed to make it better?"

"Maybe, he thought he had to send you flowers to apologize. You are kinda hard to talk to when you're mad. Maybe, this was his way of softening you up," Lewis reasoned, unsure why he was defending Derek.

"Hard to talk to? You're damn right! Fuck him if he thinks I'm talking to him after this! Like what the fuck are you even sorry for? All that worry that I had has gone to shit, and I'm fucking pissed!" Taryn broke out.

"Well, can we be pissed and not injure ourselves physically by sitting in broken glass?" Lewis said softly, gesturing to the shattered vase around them. "Please?"

With a nod, Taryn let him help her up from the ground. Her body was frozen again as he shrugged off his jacket and began using it to dust the shards of glass from her slacks. Grabbing her arm and helping her to a desk away from the glass, she slumped down into the chair, seemingly mentally exhausted.

"Let me get you home," Lewis said.

"But the glass," Taryn retorted, her attention now on the glass decorating the floor of the room as the clean freak in her refused to let her walk away from the mess she had just made. "I'm such a fucking idiot."

Shaking her head, Taryn got up and started to pick the small pieces of glass off the floor, clenching the broken pieces in one hand as she frantically tried to the clean the mess. Lewis rushed to her side again, taking the broken glass from her hand as he saw thick droplets of dark red blood coming from cuts that now covered her hands.

"Stop. I got it," Lewis said. "Go wash your hands, and I'll take care of this. Go."

"But…" Taryn started to argue.

"Now," he said sternly, refusing to take no for an answer.

As Taryn walked out of the room, Lewis looked around at the horror scene in front of him. The shards of glass seemed to symbolize Taryn, broken and scattered to a point that he wasn't sure was fixable anymore. She tried to pick herself up, put herself together again, no matter how much blood and tears it would cost her. But then this Derek guy just waltzed into her life, shattering her even further. How was she going to heal if this new guy was only going to break her more? The protective instincts over Taryn began to take over as Lewis let out a heavy sigh and shook his head, making a silent promise to himself to protect his friend from further heartache at all costs.

13

Taryn

Lewis had cleaned up the classroom to perfection, somehow not cutting himself once on the broken glass before driving Taryn home. As she sat soaking in her tub, she could hear Nathan and Lewis talking in the kitchen. Their voices drifting to her like a distant nightmare.

"Derek sent her the flowers?" Nathan asked.

"Yes, and it set her off. Rage took over, and she smashed the entire vase into the ground," Lewis stated.

"And she cut herself with the glass?" Nathan continued.

"Not on purpose. She knelt down in the broken shards before trying to clean it up. Her mind was just not there." Lewis sighed. "I don't know what to do. Have you heard from Derek?"

"He called this morning after I called his sister. She found him at their parents' house and ripped into him for me," Nathan explained.

"What did he say?" Lewis asked.

"He told me what happened, tried to explain himself to me. But I told him I didn't want to hear it. He owed Taryn an explanation, not me. I guess that's when he ordered her the flowers," Nate tried to reason to himself.

"Why didn't he just call her?" Lewis wondered.

"He said he had to talk to her in person or something but he needed to apologize first." Nate sighed.

Frustrated listening in on their conversation, Taryn got up, wrapped a towel around herself, and walked into the kitchen to confront them.

"I can hear you guys, you know?" she seethed.

"Ti," Lewis replied in shock, thinking their conversation was quiet enough to not reach her ears.

"Why did you break the glass?" Nate snapped, ignoring her question.

"Because I was mad, and I just lost it, okay? After everything I've been through, this has been a long time coming," Taryn retorted coldly. "And I think that my little breakdown was a lot healthier than other shit I could have done."

"Taryn, don't talk stupid," Lewis argued.

"No! I'm sick of trying to be perfect and hold my shit together. I feel like crapping on the world right now. The divorce, losing my mother-in-law, my student's suicide, and now Derek's bullshit? I think anyone else in my shoes would've stuck the barrel of a gun down their mouth at this point. I just broke a stupid fucking vase, so give me a damn break," she seethed.

"Ti." Nathan sighed. "We get it. We just want to be here for you and don't know how. I don't want you shutting down again like you did after the divorce. But I also don't want you breaking down like today where you hurt yourself. Even if it was an accident. What can we do to help?" he said, his voice drenched in sincerity and concern for his sister.

"Honestly?" she yelled before her voice broke in her throat and sobs slipped past her lips as she collapsed to her knees, dropping her head. "*I don't know.*"

Lewis knelt down in front of her and pulled her into his chest, shushing her as he rocked back and forth.

"I don't know either, Ti. Just know we're here for you. Whatever you need, you just tell us, okay?" Lewis whispered gently into her hair.

"If Derek's the reason why you end up in the deep end, I'm going to kill him," Nathan said through clenched teeth.

"No, you're not. He's not our concern. Taryn is. And we're going to be here for her," Sienna interjected as she walked in the front door, overhearing the conversation. Walking over to Nathan, she placed a loving hand on his back and rubbed comfort into him. "Now, Taryn, let's get you up. I got her, boys."

Sienna walked over to Taryn, pulled her from Lewis's arms, and walked her back into her room. The boys were left to deal with their testosterone alone in the kitchen. Sienna helped Taryn back into her tub. Taking each of her hands, Sienna used a tweezer from the counter to make sure all the glass was out, before she started gently rubbing off the dried blood.

"So Derek, huh?" Sienna said on a sigh.

"Yeah. He sent me flowers," Taryn said emotionless.

"That's nice of him. It's the least he could do after ghosting you." Sienna scoffed.

"I destroyed them." Taryn's face was solemn.

"Oh. That works too." Sienna giggled. "You do whatever you need to so you feel better. If you needed to destroy something to get some anger out, by all means do it."

"I do feel better now." Taryn laughed. "Thank you."

"Anytime." Sienna smiled. "You okay?"

"I will be," Taryn said on a sigh. "I always am."

Suddenly, a sick feeling overwhelmed Taryn as she shot up from the tub, pushed past Sienna, and ran for the toilet. Her knees meeting the coolness of the tile just as her body purged the contents of her stomach into the toilet. Unsure of what was going on, Sienna grabbed a towel and dropped it over Taryn's back, holding her hair from her face as the heaves kept coming. In this moment, Sienna's heart ached for Taryn. She was the strongest woman Sienna knew, but here, kneeling naked in a fetal position over the toilet, she looked like a fragile glass doll on the verge of shattering into a million pieces.

"Taryn?" Sienna asked once the heaving subsided. "Are you okay?"

"I don't know. I just... I don't feel sick. Maybe, it was something I ate," Taryn reasoned.

"What did you eat today?" Sienna questioned with genuine concern.

"I had a coffee and instant oatmeal for breakfast that Lewis grabbed me from McDonald's and then Mel's for lunch. But I've never had an issue with the food from either places before, and if I'm sick, Lewis should be sick too. We ate the same thing," Taryn thought aloud, confused.

"Taryn?" Sienna stated with worry, thinking back to Taryn throwing up at the airport. "When was the last time you had your period?"

"Huh?" Taryn said, pulling the towel around her.

"When was the last time you had your period?" Sienna repeated.

Taryn's face froze as her mind seemed to race to recall the date of her last period. Was it in May? No. She had finished it the last week of April before they flew up for Nathan's graduation in May. She remembered because she was excited that she wouldn't have to worry about bringing pads with her on their trip.

"Oh no." Taryn's chest started to rise and fall rapidly as she panicked in disbelief. "I can't be."

"What, Taryn? Talk to me" Sienna pushed, eyes wide and waiting impatiently.

"I didn't get my period in May. I usually get it at the end of the month, but I didn't." Taryn started to hyperventilate, it was her eyes that were wide now as her mind raced with realization.

"Have you and Derek been using protection?" Sienna asked seriously.

Thinking back, Taryn closed her eyes and sighed heavily. Each time they had sex, it was unplanned, spur of the moment, and since she was on birth control and had PCOS, it was difficult for her to even get pregnant to begin with. She didn't take condoms into consideration with Derek at all. Fuck! What was she thinking?

"No." Taryn sighed as tears welled in her eyes.

"Taryn!" Sienna exclaimed.

"Shhh! Between my PCOS and being on birth control, this wasn't likely to happen. And even so, we don't even know if I really am pregnant! I can't be. It's nearly impossible with those two things combined. Right?" Taryn tried to reason and calm herself down.

"I'll go to the store and get you a test. You can take it tonight after Nathan and I go to bed," Sienna offered.

"Thank you." Taryn smiled, her eyes glazing over.

"Don't worry, I won't tell Nathan. He already wants to kill Derek. I don't want him to have more reason to do so," Sienna replied. "Just don't worry until you take the test tonight, okay?"

"Okay. I'll get cleaned up in here, and I'll meet you outside for dinner." Taryn smiled. "Thank you again, Sienna."

Lewis had already left by the time Taryn came out of the bathroom. Nathan was on his laptop, two pizza boxes were placed on the counter, and Sienna had used the excuse that her sister needed help with something really quick to run off to the drugstore for the pregnancy test. As Taryn opened the box to grab a slice of pepperoni, the smell of the marinara sauce made her stomach turn, and her mouth water with sour spit. She closed the box quickly and headed over to the fridge for a glass of water.

"Pssst. Here," Sienna said, slipping back into the apartment. "Take it before Nathan comes out of the room."

"Thank you, Sienna," Taryn whispered as she took the purple box from her.

"What the fuck is that?" Nathan's voice boomed across the room to the women in the kitchen. Both of them froze in place as Taryn rushed to hide the box behind her back.

"It's pizza, babe. Didn't you buy it?" Sienna tried to play off, opening the white box on the counter. "Smells so good. Doesn't it, Ti?"

"Yep," Taryn said, trying to hold her breath. But it was too late. The smell of marinara sauce invaded her nose. Turning to the side, her face found the sink, and she vomited the water she had just drank. Sienna and Nathan's eyes grew wide as they stared in shock at Taryn. Instinctively, he rushed over to his sister, offering her a napkin when he saw the box of pregnancy tests gripped in her hand as she braced herself on the countertop.

"You're pregnant?" Nate asked in shock. Now he was the one frozen.

With the heaves still coming, Sienna answered for Taryn. "We're not sure if she is. That's what the tests are for."

"But how? Who? When?" Nathan began to stutter.

"Sex. Derek. I'm not sure," Taryn answered sarcastically into the sink between dry heaves.

"Fuck off, Ti. I'm being serious," Nate seethed.

"So am I," Taryn retorted, standing up and wiping the corners of her mouth. "Can I just pee on these sticks please before we all freak out more?"

"Go, I'll wash down the sink," Sienna said.

Nathan followed his sister into her bathroom.

"What are you doing?" Taryn scoffed.

"Waiting for you to take that damn test so I know if I need to lose my mind or not," Nathan said.

"Why? I promise it's not yours," Taryn said sarcastically.

"Yeah, but if you are and it is Derek's, I'm going to beat his ass. Then I'm going to tell Lewis and send him to beat Derek's ass again," Nathan barked.

"Well, if I am, that's what your plan is? To add more stress to me that I don't need? Really?" Taryn said wide-eyed with sass. "If it is positive, Nate, then please tell me now so I know whether or not I'm just going to lie to you."

"Huh! Just pee on the fucking stick!" Nathan yelled.

"Fuck you," Taryn said, closing the toilet cover and sitting, crossing her arms in front of her chest.

"Huh! Sienna! Come get your sister! She's driving me crazy!" Nathan called out.

"Leave her alone, Nate. Let her pee in peace! Once we find the results, then we can talk about what we're going to do. And whatever it is, *we* are going to respect and support Taryn's decisions," Sienna said as she entered the bathroom on a huff.

"Whatever, just pee already!" Nathan exclaimed again, storming out of her bathroom and plopping himself on the edge of Taryn's bed.

Taking all four tests out of the box, Taryn made quick work of peeing on all of them just to double- and triple-check. Covering the ends and setting them on the counter, it was now a waiting game. The next five minutes couldn't go by fast enough.

14

Derek

The entire week had passed, and he still had not heard from Taryn. He knew she got the flowers because he made sure to have Emma call Nathan and check, but he knew Taryn would not talk to him that easily. He still wasn't ready to go back to the Bay, and knowing his close ties to Lexie, his producer gave him a few more days off to pull himself together. They started production again on Sunday and expected him back to work by Saturday, at the end of the week. However, he had to go back and face Taryn. Whatever was left to face after fucking up yet again. So he flew up two days before he was expected back. He figured getting in on Thursday would give him a chance to surprise her at the university, maybe watch her lecture a class, and then spend the entire afternoon making it up to her if she'd let him. Derek was nervous as he arrived at USF.

After asking around where her class was, he found himself standing outside of a large mahogany door, with a little glass window to look in at her. He smiled to himself, feeling like he was at a zoo as he saw her in her natural habitat, interacting and laughing with students, the excitement on her face when someone said something wonderful made him smile to himself. He could have stood there and watched her all day.

"Can I help you?" a deep voice asked from behind him.

"Yes, I'm here for Taryn. I just didn't want to interrupt her lecture," Derek replied nonchalantly, briefly glancing back at the man standing behind him.

"Sorry. I didn't catch your name," the man said with a cautious smile, sticking his hand out for Derek to shake. His forearm was showered in tribal tattoos with a sense of familiarity.

"I'm Derek," he said with a smile, shaking the man's hand.

The demeanor on the man's face suddenly changed into a scowl as he squeezed down hard on Derek's hand. "YOU'RE DEREK?" he seethed through clenched teeth.

"Yes," Derek replied apprehensively, yanking his hand back. "You are?"

"I'm Lewis. Taryn's friend." Lewis seemed to grow in place as he squared his shoulders in front of Derek, his chest heaving as anger seeped from his pores.

"Oh," was all Derek could say as he looked at this monstrous man standing before him. Derek now understood why one punch from this guy could have knocked Taryn nearly unconscious.

"I think you should leave," Lewis said venomously.

"I need to talk to Taryn," Derek tried to reason, not wanting to set off her new guard dog. "Wait, are you here to see her too?"

"Not that it's your business, but I'm in her class. She was feeling nauseous again, so she sent me to her office to grab her more ginger candies," Lewis retorted. "But again, you should leave. She doesn't want to talk to you."

"I just need five minutes with her. I just want to explain myself." Derek sighed frustratedly.

"You have no right to demand anything from her!" Lewis barked, leaning down into Derek's face.

Lewis's tone shot through the door and immediately got Taryn's attention. Rushing to the door, she pushed it open before quickly closing the door behind her. Taryn suddenly found herself standing in between two very angry men. Closing her eyes and taking a deep breath, she centered herself.

"Enough. Not here. Lewie, please go inside. I'll be right in, promise," Taryn said sternly.

"You sure?" Lewis asked, not taking his piercing eyes from Derek.

"Positive," she replied. "Thank you."

On a huff, Lewis turned on his heels and headed into the class, slamming the door behind him.

"Please leave," Taryn said, turning to Derek.

"Taryn, please," he pleaded, turning into mush in front of her. The cold emptiness of her eyes shot fear into him. Was he too late? Did he lose her?

"No. Fool me once, shame on you. Fool me twice, shame on me. I'm done. Please leave before I call security," Taryn said coldly before turning to walk away.

Derek's arms shot out and wrapped around her body, holding her in place as he dropped to his knees, tears welling in his eyes. Kneeling before her, refusing to let her go, he didn't care who saw him.

"I know I messed up. I know I should've called you. I didn't want to burden you with my own crap. I'm sorry, Ti. I'm sorry. Please don't leave me," Derek begged between sobs.

Taryn remained silent as they remained there, her breathing steady.

"You need to leave," she said slowly, emphasizing each word. "Goodbye, Derek." Taryn pushed his arms from her waist and shrugged him off. Without looking back, she opened the door to her class and locked it behind her, leaving Derek a mess on his knees in the university hallway.

15

Taryn

In the safety of her classroom, Taryn locked the door behind her and leaned on it for support, the coolness of the wood meeting her back. She clenched her eyes shut and took a deep breath. The classroom was still with silence as all her students, including Lewis, sat on the edge of their seats, waiting to see what Taryn would do next. Opening her eyes, they were glazed over with tears, threatening to pour from her body.

"Unofficial lesson when it comes to building relationships with your students? The more transparent you are with them, opening up to them, the more they'll trust you and be willing to learn from you. It makes you human." She sighed, her voice cracking as she gave a half smile, letting a single tear drop from her eyes.

"Are you okay, Ms. Ti?" Sylvia asked.

"No, I'm not. This past year has been the roughest of my life, and this job was a godsend. It gave me an escape from the troubles back home. Still, new issues found me here. But that's life, right?" Taryn said softly as she walked to the front of the classroom. "Close your laptops, put your books away. We're going to talk story."

"Talk story?" Tanner questioned. "Is it like storytelling that you want us to do on the fly?"

"It's the Hawai'i way to say '*chat*.' I told you guys the best way to connect with your students is to be transparent with them and let them know you're human. So it's about time I get transparent with you guys," Taryn said with a smile, sitting down on the edge of her desk.

Her students followed her instructions as she popped a ginger candy into her mouth, nodding her thanks to Lewis who stood beside her desk protectively. On a heavy sigh, she spilled her heart out to her students, bringing some of them to tears. She told them about the divorce, the death of her mother-in-law, the death of her student, and the mess she was in with Derek.

"I don't even know how you're here, Ms. Ti? With all of that? I wouldn't be able to handle it," Sylvia said, wiping her eyes.

"I don't know how I'm here either. But what I keep telling myself is there's a reason for me to go through all of this, and I'm actually lucky. Some of my freshman back home have it way worse, so who am I to complain, you know? You just gotta keep your head held high and take it a day at a time." Taryn sighed. "It's just like teaching. Every day in the class is going to be different. New challenges will be thrown at you, and the second you find balance, you fall off another cliff. But you can't give up. You push through and be a role model to your students, showing them that despite difficult times, you can get back up and move forward in your life."

"So are you pregnant now?" Tanner asked randomly, causing Taryn to stiffen up. She was hoping they weren't paying attention to that part of the story. "Is that why Lewie keeps getting you those ginger candies? To help with the nausea from the morning sickness?"

Taryn sighed heavily, looking to Lewis, trying to figure out what to say next before turning to the class.

"Yes, I am." She sighed heavily, with a half-hearted smile, trying not to cry. "All four tests came out positive, and I have an appointment tomorrow to confirm with the doctors."

"And Derek is the…" Sylvia started.

A loud bang on the door cut her off and startled the entire class as their attention was drawn to sad hazel eyes staring through the glass window.

"You're pregnant?" Derek yelled through the door. His eyes began filling with tears, not caring how crazed he looked or if he was crying in front of her entire class of students.

Lewis's body tensed next to her, and heat radiated from him as anger began to build.

"He was out there this whole time? I thought you told him to leave?" Lewis seethed, his fists clenching.

"I did tell him to leave. This is a fucking mess!" Taryn snapped, bringing the eyes of her students back up front to where she stood. Taking a deep breath, she gathered strength. "Class, we'll pick this up next week. Have a good weekend. Don't forget your homework, okay? Email me if you need help."

With that, the class exited the front door, pushing past Derek and forcing him to stand to the side until it was only Taryn and Lewis in the classroom. Silently, Lewis gathered Taryn's belongings as Derek walked in hesitantly, his chest heaving, sobs still slipping from his lips. His eyes were burning holes into Taryn, demanding answers.

"You're pregnant?" he finally uttered, his voice shaking.

"What the fuck do you care!" Lewis seethed.

"Lew, it's okay. I'm fine," Taryn said, grabbing his forearm to calm him. "Give me five minutes, and I'll meet you at the car, Lewie."

Lewis hesitated, standing there looking between Derek and Taryn, unsure if he should leave. After seeing the determination in Taryn's eyes, he let out a heavy sigh and grabbed the last of their belongings from the desk.

"Call me if you need me to come back for you, okay?" Lewis replied, kissing her on the head as he left the class. His eyes were silently stabbing Derek as he passed. "She comes out crying, I'm coming back for your head," he threatened on a low whisper.

Soon, it was just Taryn and Derek in the empty classroom, the tension thick and suffocating them. Derek, unsure of what to do or say, simply stood there and stared at her, his appearance disheveled, shadowy scruff from his beard growing in, making him look worn down. His eyes were glassy from crying.

"Are you pregnant?" Derek asked, his voice shaking.

84

"Yes." Taryn's answer was short and cold as she tried to maintain her own composure. She refused to cry in front of him. Not for her own sake but for his, knowing that Lewis would follow through on his threat to protect her.

Derek swallowed hard, his breath shallow as he blinked rapidly. "Is…is it mine?" he finally asked.

"Do you want it to be?" Taryn retorted harshly.

Shock filled his face. He had no idea how to talk to this Taryn who was so on guard, distant, and cold toward him. His body language looked as if it were fighting itself from throwing his arms around her but afraid to step any closer.

"I'll take your lack of response as a 'no.' Have a good life, Derek," Taryn scoffed as she began walking toward the door, maneuvering herself around him to pass. Her shoulder brushed his arm, bringing him back to life. His hand shot out and grasped her wrist, stopping her in her tracks.

"Taryn, I love you," Derek pleaded.

"Disappearing on someone shows love," she scoffed, letting out a sarcastic sigh.

"Ti, I was crazed and stupid. I didn't want to dump my shit on you. But I realized you are the only person I need in my life." Derek's voice began to shake.

"Well, you got a funny way of showing it," Taryn argued, trying to yank her hand free. "Derek, please let me go."

"No! I'm not going to let you just walk out of my life. I love you, Taryn! I Love You! Please!" Derek stepped in front of her, taking her hands in his and bending down, forcing her to look him in the eyes. "Taryn, I love you," he whispered into her face.

"I can't do this Derek. This back and forth. I just can't," her voice began to crack. "I'm done."

"Is this baby mine?" Derek touched her tummy gently with one hand as he held his breath for her answer.

They seemed to be frozen in time as they stood there, neither of them speaking. Was this it for them?

16

Derek

Derek's answer from Taryn never came. Shrugging him off and pushing past him without another word, she stormed out to the parking lot. He froze. His heart shattering, and his world falling apart, before his mind could even comprehend what was happening. Suddenly, his feet took action for him, chasing after her, but it was too late. Derek caught a glimpse of her sprinting to the car. Lewis was waiting for her with the door open as she jumped in. Derek ran full blast toward her, willing for her to wait as tears blurred his vision. In the blink of an eye, the car was gone, Lewis speeding off down the street. Derek had pushed her away when he needed her the most, and now he'd lost her completely.

"Fuck!" he yelled to the sky as he dropped to his knees in the dewy grass. Pulling his phone out, he dialed Taryn frantically. Each time, his call was immediately forwarded to voice mail. Desperate, he called Nathan.

"What do you want?" Nathan spat over the phone.

"Can you please tell Taryn to call me?" Derek begged.

"She doesn't have to do anything she doesn't want to," Nathan retorted harshly.

"Nathan, is that baby mine?" Derek sobbed.

"What do you care? You're only going to disappear and run away when shit gets hard," Nathan seethed.

"Nate, please. I do care. I love her, and if that's my baby, I promise I won't fuck up again," Derek pleaded.

"I don't believe you," Nathan scoffed. "That's Taryn's baby. It's my niece or nephew. If you have anything to do with it, you were just the sperm donor. Nothing more because when you really love someone, you don't just fucking run away when you feel bad for yourself. You man up, deal with your shit, and you be there for the people you claim to care about. The people you claim to love."

With that, Nathan hung up on Derek. He was running out of options. The only thing he could think to do was go to her apartment and wait for her to come home. She had to go there eventually, right? There was nowhere else for her to go. Running to his car and speeding toward her apartment, he yanked his car into park in front of the driveway to her building, his eyes searching for her.

"She won't be back until Monday," Sienna's voice rang through his window with sass, pulling Derek's attention to the sidewalk and prompting him to get out of his car.

"Where could she have gone?" Derek began to panic.

"Why should I tell you?" Sienna scoffed.

"Sienna, I know you hate me..." he started.

"Well, that's the understatement of the year," she said sarcastically, rolling her eyes.

"But I do love her. It took me hitting rock bottom to realize how much I need her in my life. Please!" Derek begged.

"I'm only telling this because you look fucking pathetic, okay? She's at Lewis's place up near Sacramento." Sienna huffed with irritation.

"Lewis?" he questioned, his heart racing in his chest.

"Uh, did I stutter?" Sienna retorted. "Yes, Lewis. Her friend from back home. He has his own house about an hour south from the army base out there. Taryn didn't want to risk you doing this because she wants some damn space from you, so she asked if she could stay in his guest room for a bit." Shaking her head, she turned toward the entrance to the apartment building.

"Taryn's pregnant," Derek started.

"Uh-huh." Sienna nodded, punching in the code to the building without looking back.

"Is the baby mine?" Derek asked. "Or is it Lewis's?" Derek's heart stopped as he waited for an answer. What he got from Sienna was unexpected. She turned slowly, anger radiating from her body as she faced him. Her eyes were like daggers as her fists clenched at her sides and her chest heaved, her rage on the verge of exploding.

"Are you fucking serious? Really? *You're* going to play the jealousy card? Other than Nathan, Lewis has been the *only guy* who has been there for her to pick up the pieces you keep taping together before shattering her apart over and over again. He's her *friend*! Taryn isn't a slut if that's what you're suggesting," Sienna yelled, getting in his face.

"I just figured I'd ask. They used to fool around a while ago. And well, she did sleep with me on the first night," Derek retorted hesitantly.

"They fooled around *over ten years ago*! She doesn't even see him like that anymore. And as for her sleeping with you the first night? You were the first person she opened up to about her ex-husband before she even told her family anything, mind you! She's *only* been with *you*! She loves *you*! Although I don't see why. You're a fucking idiot! How dare you accuse her of that when you were the one caught sucking face with your ex. You were the one who disappeared after running to your ex's family! How fucking dare you!" Sienna was practically screaming at him on the street, and for a petite Korean girl, she had him cowering.

"So the baby is mine?" Derek smiled in relief.

"Yes, You Fucking Idiot! The baby is yours!" Sienna exclaimed, frustrated as she turned and stormed off toward the building.

"Thank you," he called after her before turning into his car and pulling away from the sidewalk.

As he drove back to his apartment, an array of emotions was overcoming him. He was worried about Taryn, mad at himself for putting them in this situation, but he was also happy that she was carrying his baby. Derek was going to be a dad, and he was ecstatic about it. Now, he just had to get Taryn back so they could be a family. Somehow, he had to make this right. But how?

17

Taryn

Sitting at the dinner table in Lewis's farmhouse, Taryn couldn't help but smile at little Kam sitting there eating her grapes. For dinner, Lewis had made beef stew and fruit salad as they were the only things that even sounded appetizing to Taryn at the moment. Kam was more than delighted when Lewis told her that Taryn would be staying with them for a little while. After explaining what was going on to Elaine, she had taken Taryn under her wing to help her with her pregnancy. She was the one who told Taryn about the ginger candies to help with the nausea. As she sat at the table, Taryn was filled with gratitude for still being blessed enough to have such amazing people in her life despite what she had been through.

"Aunty Ti? Want to watch *Frozen* with me after we shower?" Kam's tiny voice asked over the table.

"Of course! I love *Frozen*." Taryn smiled.

"And we can drive Daddy crazy singing!" Kam laughed. "You can sing Anna's part, and I can be Elsa!"

"Not more singing, Kam, or I'm going to end up signing the songs randomly at work again and get bullied by the other guys," Lewis said, pouting.

"But, Daddy, it always makes me feel happy. And Aunty Ti needs to be happy right now. Please, Daddy?" Kam begged with a little pout.

"Okay." Lewis sighed, giving in.

It was so weird to see Lewis go from playboy to father. But he was badass at it. It was as if becoming a father had finally made Lewis whole. Taryn was floored with happiness for him as she watched him interact with his daughter. Kam mimicking how Lewis ate, Lewis brushing her hair, and even painting her nails as they watched *Frozen*. Lewis was an amazing dad. After Kam fell asleep, he carried her to bed and tucked her in.

"It's the best feeling in the world," he whispered to Taryn as he joined her in the doorway of Kam's room, both of them looking at her tiny body asleep in this huge pink princess bed.

"I hope so," Taryn whispered sighing heavily. "Do you think I'm doing the right thing? Not letting Derek be involved?"

"Ti, I can't answer that. You need to do what's right for you. But let us go to Elaine's doctor tomorrow, and then once it's confirmed that you're pregnant, from more than just sticks, you can figure out how involved you want to let Derek be, okay?" Lewis said, putting an arm around Taryn's shoulder and pulling her into his chest. Kissing her on the head, he added, "But whatever happens, know we got you, and we'll make sure it all works out okay. I promise."

"Thanks, Lewie." She sighed, wrapping her arm around his waist, hugging him. "What would I do without you?"

"Honestly? I don't know," he teased. "But can I tell you something I do know?" Taryn nodded into his chest, encouraging him to continue. "If I weren't able to be in Kam's life, it would've killed me. Just think about that before you shut Derek out completely, okay?"

"I thought you hated him?" Taryn pulled back, confused, unsure of what that's supposed to mean.

"I do hate him. But I'm also a dad, Taryn. And as a dad, it would kill me if I couldn't be in my kid's life, and I feel for anyone who can't be involved or see their kid grow up." He sighed. "I lucked out with Elaine in that sense. We've really gotten good at co-parenting, and we've become amazing friends raising Kam together this way."

As she lay in bed in his guest room that night, she couldn't stop thinking about what Lewis said. If she really was pregnant, she had a huge decision to make. Would it be worse to keep Derek out of her kid's life? Or is it worse to let him in only for him to run away from them both this time?

*****

The OB-GYN office was cold, sterile. Feeling uncomfortable with being in the room, Lewis waited outside with Kam while Elaine went in with Taryn. She was instructed to put on a hospital gown and take off her panties, wrapping herself in this weird paperlike cloth.

"I feel so exposed," Taryn said softly to Elaine.

"Get used to it, girl. When you give birth, there's a team of people in there. You can't be ashamed of anything." Elaine smiled, giving Taryn a comforting rub on her arm.

"So how does this work?" Taryn asked nervously.

"Well, the doctor will come in, check your cervix, and then he'll do an ultrasound with…" Elaine began.

A knock at the door interrupted her as it swung open gently, pulling Elaine's attention to the doorway. A look of confusion furrowed her brow.

"You're not the doctor?" Elaine questioned to whoever was standing behind Taryn's head, out of her field of vision.

"I know. I'm the father," Derek's voice rang in Taryn's ears, sucking the breath from her lungs.

"Derek?" Elaine questioned, angrily crossing her arms over her chest. Her eyes narrowed. "I heard about you."

Taryn could hear Derek's footsteps as he entered the room, circling the bed until he was standing to the side of her. He looked as if he hadn't slept all night. His eyes were puffy and red, his hair was a mess, and he was in the same clothes he was wearing yesterday. Taryn tried to maintain her composure as he stood there, refusing to back down. Despite the disheveled appearance, was he smiling?

"What are you doing here?" Taryn finally asked, turning to look at him. "How did you even know I was here?"

"I called him," Lewis' voice echoed in the room as he emerged in the doorway, Kam in tow behind him.

"What? Why? How could you do this to me, Lewie?" Taryn was on the verge of tears as her friend approached the side of the bed, opposite of Derek.

"Lewis, I told you not to call him. It has to be Taryn's choice!" Elaine jumped in, defending an overly exposed and overly emotional Taryn laying on the doctor's table, vulnerable in the middle of the mess.

"Ti, I know you're pissed at me right now, but we shouldn't be here. It should be you and Derek," Lewis started, motioning between himself and Elaine. "I took his number from your phone when you were showering last night to tell him to leave you alone for good. But after talking to him, he really does love you, Taryn. More importantly? He wants to be here for you *and* the baby. Not a lot of guys nowadays are willing to do that. So, please, give him another chance."

Taryn lay there silently, tears streaming down her cheeks, unsure of what to do and hating that she was feeling forced into this situation. She was always in control of her life, so to have everyone making decisions for her was too much for her hormonal emotions to take. Taryn understood why Lewis did this, but it was too much for her to take right now.

"Ti, I know you. Being cold like this? It isn't you. You know I love you, and I will always have your back. But for once, will you trust someone other than yourself?" Lewis added as he leaned down and kissed Taryn on the forehead. "We'll give you two some privacy. Just give me a call later when you're ready to talk okay? I'm sorry."

"It's okay, Aunty. We love you," Kam said, her tiny voice carrying over the table, her little arms taking Taryn's and squeezing it with a hug. Despite how young she was, it was as if she understood and tried to soften the blow of Lewis dropping the Derek bomb on her.

"Thank you, sweetie." Taryn sighed, trying to stay strong in front of Lewis's little girl. Elaine and Lewis exited the room, Kam in tow. The door closed with a soft thud behind them, Taryn's eyes stayed glued to the ceiling, tears silently falling from the corners as she tried to comprehend what just happened.

"I'm sorry he forced you into this. He told me you knew I was coming," Derek tried to reason, his voice pulling her back to the present.

"It's okay. He knows if he told me, I wouldn't have come here at all. I would've run if I knew he was setting this shit up," Taryn said, her voice shallow, refusing to look at him.

Gently taking her hand, Derek gave it a quick squeeze before she yanked it from his grasp, seemingly yanking his heart from his chest simultaneously. Unsure of how else to get her attention, he leaned over her, blocking her view of the ceiling tiles and forcing her to look at him. His eyes were watering, and his shoulders started to rise and fall rapidly, sobs slipping from his lips. Her eyes unwillingly met his, breaking his heart with the emptiness there as she stared up at him.

"I know I hurt you, and you have every right to be mad at me, to not trust me right now. But I'm so sorry, Taryn. I'm *so* sorry. I love you so much. Please, let me be here for you and our baby," he started. "I know I don't deserve another chance, and you have every right to throw me out of this room right now, but I beg you, please let me take care of the two of you." Derek started crying, his tears burning Taryn's cheek as she dropped her head to the side, his hand moving from the bed to rest on her tummy and hold her hand. "Even if you're weren't pregnant, I promise, I am never leaving you again. I know it was a mistake running in the first place, but if you'll have me, I'll stand by your side until I take my last breath. Just…please, Taryn, please."

More tears began to fall from Taryn's eyes. She had no words to say, no way to respond to him. The battle between her heart aching for him and her head telling her to walk away was killing her slowly inside. Suddenly, she was saved by the doctor who came in with a smile.

"Am I interrupting?" she asked gently.

"No, Doctor. We're fine. We're just talking." Taryn forced a smile, wiping her tears and sitting up.

Derek moved to the opposite side of her, silent but still clenching her hand in his as if it were the only thing holding him to the earth.

"I'm Doctor Matsuda. My patient, Elaine, tells me we might be pregnant?" she said, sitting down and putting on gloves with a smile. "I'm just going to check your cervix really quick, and we'll get that ultrasound going, okay?"

The doctor moved down to the end of the table, using one hand to prompt Taryn to spread her thighs. Derek watched the doctor like a hawk, making sure she was being gentle with Taryn. As the doctor's fingers entered Taryn, feeling around inside of her, Taryn's body tensed as she held her breath. Derek instinctively squeezed her hand and glared at the doctor.

"You're hurting her," he seethed softly.

"No, she's just a little sensitive right now. That's usually a sign of pregnancy," the doctor calmed with an understanding smile.

From there, the doctor lifted Taryn's hospital gown up, exposing her tummy. Doctor Matsuda squeezed a dollop of jelly onto Taryn's tummy, causing her to shiver.

"Are you okay?" Derek asked, worried.

"It's just cold." Taryn sighed.

Turning off the lights, the doctor flipped on a computer screen as she rolled it closer to the edge of the bed. With a little wand, she started moving it around Taryn's tummy. A little triangle-looking thing popped up on the screen, causing Taryn and Derek to tilt their heads in confusion, as a loud whooshing pulsing beat echoed in the room.

"What are we looking at, Doc?" Derek asked.

"Well, that's your tummy," she said, outlining the triangle on the screen with her free hand. "And that, this little peanut-looking thing…is your baby. Congratulations, you two. You're going to be parents," she finished, pointing toward the bottom of the screen with a smile.

"I'm pregnant?" Taryn asked, shocked. "Like I'm really pregnant?" Tears of joy began to fill her eyes.

"I'll give you guys a minute," Doctor Matsuda said, freezing the image on the screen and leaving the room to give them privacy.

"That's our baby." Derek smiled. He kissed Taryn's knuckles, both of them gazing at the screen.

"That's our baby," she repeated, smiling.

18

Derek

Derek was ecstatic. He had never felt happier in his entire life. He didn't know if he was ready to be a father, but with Taryn by his side for the journey, he would have been ready for anything. As he drove them back to San Francisco, Taryn remained quiet, staring out at the scenery and the city lights as they crossed over the Bay Bridge.

"Are you hungry?" Derek asked hesitantly.

"I guess." Taryn sighed.

"What are you craving?" he asked.

"I don't know," she replied. "I just know I can't go to Italian restaurants right now. For some reason, the baby doesn't like marinara sauce."

"Really? That's the complete opposite of you. Your favorite food is Italian, right?" Derek smiled.

"How'd you know that? I never told you that," Taryn said, tilting her head at Derek.

"Well, beautiful," he started, taking her hand in his and kissing her knuckles, "I'm an observer, and based on the dishes you like to cook and what you like to order from UberEATS, it's always your go to. Next to soup dumplings that is."

"You really do pay attention." She sighed, shocked, unable to pull her hand away from his. Suddenly, she exclaimed, "Ooooo! Soup dumplings!"

"I can try to find somewhere, but most dim sum places close by 2:00 p.m. The soup dumplings are kind of a breakfast food here," Derek said solemnly.

"Really?" The look on her face made Derek's heart drop. She was finally talking to him, and he was already disappointing her.

"Let me make some calls, okay? Hold on." He smiled as Taryn turned over in her seat. The excitement of the day was really taking its toll on her as she fell asleep.

Derek pulled up Annie's number in his phone. Her family owned a small dim sum restaurant on Twenty-Fourth in the Richmond district. He was hoping he could pull some strings and see if she would open up for Taryn.

"Annie? It's D!" he said when she answered with a peppy hello.

"It's D, everyone!" she exclaimed. "We just finished shooting for today. How are you doing?"

"Are you coming back tomorrow?" Ananya yelled in the background.

"Yeah, bro! We miss you" he heard Ben say.

"I'll be there tomorrow, but I have a lot to tell you, guys. Annie, do you think you could do me the biggest favor in the world?" Derek asked sweetly.

"Depends. What do you need?" Annie replied.

"Do you think you could meet us at your parents' restaurant and steam some soup dumplings for me? Please?" Derek asked meekly.

"Really, D? That's what you need?" she asked, confused.

"It's not for me. It's for... Taryn." Derek sighed.

"Taryn? She's actually talking to you? After everything you put her through?" Annie sounded shocked.

"Do you have her under some kind of spell, bro? We love you, but we all agreed we wouldn't have talked to you ever again after that disappearing act you pulled," Ben echoed in the background.

"Well, it's complicated. We kinda just need each other right now." Derek sighed, not wanting to tell them anything else.

"If she's putting up with you, I commend her. She deserves soup dumplings!" Annie said, her smile hinted in her tone. "We can all eat dinner there. Meet us in thirty?"

"Thank you, Annie! We'll be there! I owe you!" Derek sighed.

Taryn started to stir in the passenger seat as Derek looked over to her to see if she was okay. Touching her arm, it was ice-cold. With one hand, he reached in the back, grabbed his jacket, and threw it over her. It immediately settled her again as she sighed with contentment. Even asleep, she was gorgeous. If they had a daughter, man, would they be in trouble. He'd have to buy a gun to keep the boys away because she would have Taryn's beauty all over her. He smiled at the thought of them raising their baby together, maybe having another little one in the future. Taryn sat up suddenly, cold sweat on her face as she started breathing heavily.

"Derek, pull over," she panted, eyes wide.

Pulling off the road, into some street parking by the AT&T stadium, Taryn flew his car door open and leaned her head out just before a stream of vomit hit the pavement. Putting the car in park and turning on his hazards, Derek leaned over and pulled her hair back out of her face, rubbing comfort into her back. After a few more heaves, she sat back in the passenger seat. He offered her a napkin from the glove compartment that she took gratefully, wiping her mouth. The color was slowly returned to her face.

"Sorry." She sighed, guilt all over her face.

"It's okay. Here, drink some water," he said, undoing the cap on a bottle from his center console.

She sipped it as her breathing returned to normal. Taryn closed the door and motioned for Derek to drive.

"Are you okay?" Derek asked.

"Yeah, this morning sickness is a bitch." Taryn sighed as the lights of the city kissed her face.

"So can we talk?" Derek was hesitant.

"Do we have to?" Taryn sighed as she stared out the window, watching the city pass them. She was here physically with him, yet she seemed so far away.

"I would like to talk if you'll let me. I still love you, Ti, and this baby has only amplified those feelings. I want to be with you, Taryn. I want us to be a family," Derek confessed.

Taryn was silent, her face was blank. Derek didn't know what else to say, and he only had a limited time to keep her in his car to get her to listen to him. As he continued to drive, she continued to sit there without a peep.

"Taryn?" Derek finally asked as they made their way into the Richmond district. They were almost at Annie's.

"I don't know what I want." She sighed. "My head is telling me one thing, my heart another. I just don't know."

"Just tell me what you're thinking, what you're feeling right now. I can't make things better if you won't talk to me, baby." Derek sighed as he reached over, rubbing her knee.

"Don't call me that, please." Taryn sighed. "Look, I want to be with you, but I'm scared. I feel like every time we take a step forward, we end up falling a thousand steps backward. And with the baby now, I'm not sure if that's something I want to subject an innocent life to. It's been a constant tug-of-war between my head and my heart, and it can't be. This baby is my priority now. Not what I want or what I think I need or don't need."

"I know you're scared. I'm scared too. I'm scared to fuck this up again and to not be good enough for the both of you, but know that I'm going anywhere. You and our baby are the priorities in my life now." Derek pulled next to the curb, just around the block from Annie's parents' restaurant and turned off the car.

Turning to Taryn in his seat, he cupped her face lovingly with his hand, brushing a stray tear from her cheek with his thumb. "Taryn, I love you. No matter what life throws at us from here on out, I'm never leaving your side again. I will do everything in my power to be the best man to you and best father to our baby. Please, don't push me away."

They stared at each other for a while, both caught up in their array of emotions. Derek knew she was struggling, and it would be hard for her to trust him moving forward, but he would give the world, his life, down to his very last breath, to make sure Taryn and his baby were happy and taken care of.

"Taryn, I'm not asking for you to trust me or for anything more than you're willing to give. All I'm asking for is time. Please," he pleaded, feeling her slipping away from him with each second that passed. They sat in silence for what seemed like eternity.

"Fine," she said finally on a heavy sigh.

"Really?" Derek smiled.

"We'll give it this summer and go from there," she added. "But I'm not making any promises."

"Thank you, Ti." Derek cried without embarrassment, tears of relief falling from his eyes as he threw his arms around her and buried his face in her neck.

Inside of Annie's, everyone was already waiting. Three-tiered towers of woven bamboo showered a large round table near the back corner. Annie locked the door behind Taryn and Derek.

"We're so happy to see you, Taryn!" Ananya said, running up and hugging her tightly.

"My girl wants soup dumplings, I will get her soup dumplings," Derek whispered as he saw Taryn's eyes light up at the dim sum towers.

"Actually, I got her the soup dumplings," Annie said sarcastically as she hugged Taryn. "This is my parents' place. Asians. Go figure, right?" She laughed.

"Thank you so much! This this the only thing that I was craving right now." Taryn smiled gratefully.

Hearing that one word triggered everyone's eyes to turn to Taryn and Derek, wide and waiting. The air in the room seemed to be vacuumed out as mouths dropped. Derek and Taryn, the center of everyone's attention.

"Craving?" Ananya said first, cautiously looking down at Taryn's tummy. "Wait…are you?"

Taryn looked to Derek first. He nodded his approval for her to proceed and share their news. A smile spread across Taryn's face as she turned back to Ananya.

"Yeah, we just found out," Taryn said meekly.

"Ahhhh!" the girls all screamed their excitement as the boys got up from the table to shake Derek's hand in congratulations.

"Oh my gosh! The baby is going to be so cute!" Annie cried, cupping Taryn's face in her hands.

"If she pulls more on Taryn's side, she's going to be gorgeous!" Ananya added.

"Calm down, guys, we don't know what we're having, and she's only five weeks right now." Derek smiled.

"Okay, okay. I'm sorry. But still. Ahhh! So happy for you guys!" Annie smiled, wiggling with excitement.

"So? How are you feeling? I heard morning sickness sucks," Jared asked.

"It's been rough, but I think I'm okay. Just hungry." Taryn laughed as they all headed toward the table.

The rest of the conversation was light, happiness filling the room as Annie brought out an assortment of other dim sum choices so that Taryn had some options. Watching her interact with his friends, Derek smiled, contented and feeling complete again now that she was back in his life.

"Pssst... D," Ben whispered.

"Yeah?" he whispered back, leaning away from Taryn.

"You should marry her," Ben said, pointing to the ring finger on his left hand.

"What? Are you serious?" Derek whispered, surprised.

"Dude, you always say you can't see yourself with anyone else, and now you're pregnant? Just do it! You're going to be together for the rest of your life anyways," Ben reasoned seriously. "Or at least think about it. She's perfect for you, bro, and I know it'd make you happy."

His wife? Derek has once considered possibly marrying Lexie, but it was only because of their history of being together for so long. But he never did because deep down inside, he knew it would never work. Now with Taryn, it was different. He was happier with her, and he couldn't see his life without her. Even if they'd only known each other a short while, he could see himself taking that leap for her, with her. And what better way would there be to make their little family official, right? Maybe, Ben was onto something.

19

Lewis

Weeks had passed since Lewis dropped the bomb on Taryn and surprised her with Derek at her first doctor visit for the baby. After the appointment, and after Derek had gotten some food into her, Taryn was happier, allowing her and Lewis to talk everything out. She was still pissed at Lewis for what he did, but after hearing him out, she understood, and everything was right between the two of them again.

Since then, Derek, Lewis, and her brother, Nathan, had been team baby. Nathan made sure she was taken care of at home when she wasn't at the university teaching, Lewis had watch over her on days she was teaching, and Derek was to be there for her whenever he wasn't on set.

Surprisingly, Derek had actually stepped up. He even arranged his filming schedule to accommodate doctors' appointments, and he was by her side from the moment he was done on set until he had to leave her to go back. Even his castmates stepped up for him, helping to bring foods from all over the city that she was craving. Lewis was actually impressed and started to like Derek even if he would never admit it aloud.

This Thursday marked the end of classroom instruction. The next two weeks would be time to prep for their "mock classroom" projects that would take place during the last two weeks of the courses. For the curriculum development, students were to present their curriculum and teach it to the class, with their final being a reflection paper on what worked and what they would need to adjust to improve. Similarly, for the classroom management class, they would be put to the test teaching for fifteen-minute increments, with Taryn demonstrating a different behavior that could impede instruction. They would have to write a final reflection paper on how they did or what they would do differently for their final grade.

As he had been doing for the past month since classes started, Lewis pulled into the driveway of Taryn's apartment building, with a turkey sausage and egg burrito and some orange juice for her. Typically, she'd answer when he'd call, saying he's outside, but for some reason today, it kept ringing. Lewis figured she was just in the bathroom still, but when she didn't come out after fifteen minutes, he decided to head up to the apartment. Punching in the code, he went up the stairs and used the spare key from the coded safety box she installed at the base of their door.

"Taryn?" he said cautiously as he pushed the door open.

The apartment seemed empty and cold. Something felt off, and hairs on the back of Lewis's neck started to stand. He turned and entered her bedroom, still no sign of her. Going to her bathroom, the blood drained from his face, and his lungs felt as if he had been sucker punched, leaving him unable to breathe. His panic rose as adrenaline began to pump life through his body as he stared at his friend. Taryn, standing before him, had tears in her eyes, and there was blood…everywhere.

"Something's wrong," she cried, staring at Lewis for help.

20

Derek

The second he saw Lewis's name on his screen calling, he knew something bad had happened. Although he and Lewis were okay with each other, they'd typically only text. The fact that he was calling was a red flag already. Walking off set to take the call, he answered nervously.

"Hello? Lewis? Is everything okay?" Derek's voice shook.

"No. I'm taking Taryn to the emergency room right now." Lewis was breathless as if he had been running.

"What? Is she okay?" Derek began to panic.

"I don't know. I went to pick her up, and there was blood everywhere. I caught her before she hit the floor when she passed out, but she hasn't woken up yet," Lewis uttered.

"Text me what emergency room, and I'll be there," Derek rushed. "Please take care of her until I do."

"I got her, D. Don't worry. I'll keep you posted," Lewis replied before hanging up.

Derek's lungs seemed to shrivel in his chest as he leaned against the wall for support. He had to call Nathan.

"Hello?" Nate answered in his typical professional voice.

"Lewis is taking Taryn to the ER," Derek urged.

"What?" Nathan's voice changed suddenly, panicked.

"He said when he got to the apartment, there was blood everywhere, then she passed out. She's still unconscious," Derek summed.

"Okay, I'm going to have my secretary file this, and I'll be right there. What ER is she at?" Nathan sounded as if he was trying to force a sense of calm back into himself.

"Hold on, Lewis just texted," Derek said.

St. Mary's. (Lewis)

"She's at St. Mary's," Derek shared.

"Got it. See you there," Nate replied, hanging up.

Without another word, Derek sprinted to his trailer. Everyone's eyes followed him with worry. Flying the door open, he rushed to grab his jacket, backpack, and keys. Ben and Jared appeared in the doorway behind him.

"Bro, what's wrong?" Jared asked, worried.

"Taryn, they had to rush her to the ER. She's bleeding, and then she blacked out." Derek's voice began to crack, his eyes filling with tears. "I need to get to her now."

"Okay, we'll let everyone know. Call if you need anything, okay?" Jared replied.

"Thanks." Derek sighed as he gave them quick hugs and headed to the parking lot.

The drive there was tedious, a never ending stream of traffic lights and pedestrian crossings that made his journey to the hospital seem like it was taking forever. But within ten minutes, he had sped into the ER parking lot, jumped out, and was running toward her presence that was calling to him, silently pulling him toward her like a magnet.

"Please, let her be okay," Derek said to himself as he tried to hold it together. "Please. Please, let her be okay."

21

Nathan

Knowing his sister was in good hands, he stopped by the apartment to grab a few of her things in case they admitted her overnight. They had too many family members in the hospital growing up to count. So making sure she had the essentials with her was second nature to him. Nathan's eyes went wide, and his mouth dropped as he made his way through her room, stopping at the bathroom entrance with Sienna in tow behind him.

When Derek told him how Lewis described blood being everywhere, he wasn't expecting this. The white porcelain of the tub, to the toilet, the countertop, and even the floors were stained red in blood. Sienna gasped as she came up next to him. Tears immediately began stinging Nathan's eyes as worry for his sister overcame his entire being. His knees buckled, forcing him to find support against the doorframe.

"Oh my gosh," Sienna finally said. "What happened?"

"I don't know. I just need to get to her." Nathan sobbed.

"Go, I'll clean up here and have my sister drop me off to you after, okay?" Sienna said, her eyes still wide, taking in the scene in the bathroom. "Go, baby. I got it," she added, kissing his cheek and pushing him out of the bathroom toward the door.

"I'll call you," Nathan said solemnly.

His feet were suddenly taking him down the stairs and toward their car, pulling out into the street before he realized where he was going. Nathan's worry had him working in autopilot. The drive was a blur as he pulled into the hospital parking lot. Finding a stall a few down from Derek's car, he hopped out and followed the red signs to the emergency room.

Walking in, his heart dropped as he saw Derek hunched over crying helplessly, Lewis sitting next to him in silence. His eyes were red and puffy as he rubbed comfort into Derek's back. This was bad. Nathan felt frozen as the cold air of the hospital seemed to pull all life from him. Only the throbbing of his heart in his chest gave any inclination that he was still alive. This couldn't be happening. How much more tragedy could life throw at his sister?

22

Taryn

"I'm so sorry for your loss," Doctor Matsuda's words echoed over and over again in Taryn's mind. Her heart aching in her chest as she willed the darkness of her hospital room to just take her already, to swallow her whole. How could she be so hurt over something she never really had?

"Ladies with PCOS often find difficulty getting pregnant. Miscarriages are common. Please don't be discouraged," Doctor Matsuda told her.

"Did the baby feel any pain because of me?" Taryn had asked.

"No, in that stage of development, they wouldn't feel anything yet," Doctor Matsuda tried to explain.

"Is it my fault? Did I do something wrong?" Taryn cried.

"Sweetie, it's not your fault at all. The fetus just didn't attach," Doctor Matsuda tried to soothe her. "It's okay, just try and rest."

When Lewis had brought her in, said she was pregnant, and she shared her condition with the ER doctors, they immediately called Doctor Matsuda and had her come in from Sacramento. They had spent the morning poking and probing around her before showing her on the ultrasound machine that the baby wasn't there anymore. She had a miscarriage. This tiny, innocent life had been destroyed because of her fucked-up ovaries. Taryn couldn't wrap her mind around what she was feeling. The pain in her heart was incomprehensible to anything she's ever experienced in her life, and she didn't know how to deal with it.

After removing whatever it was they needed to so she didn't get sick from the chemicals in the tissues, she asked if she could be alone to rest. They decided to admit her for a few days so they could observe her and ensure everything else was okay. She had curled up in the fetal position on the bed, shut the lights off, and refused to see anyone. Taryn couldn't face anyone. Although Lewis had been there initially, she was embarrassed that she wasted his time. Knowing how happy Derek was, she was ashamed to face him, knowing it would be her fault that his happiness would be taken away. With Nathan, she didn't want to face her brother only to get his realistic lectures. She had nobody to turn to and didn't want anybody in her life right now. The only person that mattered was the baby in her tummy that she had let down before it had a chance to live. Taryn didn't know how many hours had passed, but as the sun started to rise, she heard a soft knock on her door. Not turning to see who it was, she refused to move.

"Go away please," she said softly.

Without an answer, the door pushed open, and she heard pairs of feet start patting into her room. It couldn't be the nurse because usually the nurse would say something or turn the lights on. But at this point, Taryn could care less who was there.

"Sweetie," the voice of her mother carried down into her ears, instantly filling Taryn's eyes with tears.

"Mom!" she said, sitting up suddenly and pulling her mom into a hug as she sobbed.

"My poor baby. Shhh. It's going to be okay," Tiana soothed as she rubbed Taryn on the back.

"I'm so sorry," Taryn cried.

"There's nothing to be sorry for," Tiana said, cupping her daughter's cheeks in her hands.

Taryn noticed shadows moving at the foot of her bed, and she turned her attention to them. Nathan, Sienna, Lewis, Derek, and her father, Noah, stood staring at her with empathy. Taryn felt exposed and heartbroken.

"Sweetie, nothing could have prevented this," Tiana began before continuing on a heavy sigh. "I have PCOS too. I never thought I would get pregnant, but your father and I tried and tried. And now look? We were blessed with you and your brother. It is still possible for you to be a mommy! And when you are, you'll be amazing."

"Yeah, Ti. You're going to be an amazing mom. I mean look at me? You basically helped to raise me, and I came out awesome." Nathan smiled kindly.

"And you're amazing with Kam. I think she's known you the least, but you're her favorite aunt already," Lewis added.

"It's okay to be sad right now, but you're stronger than this. You will pick yourself up and figure it out like you always do." Noah sighed, looking at his daughter.

"And we're all here for you," Tiana finished.

Taryn's eyes filled with tears as she smiled gratefully at the support system in her room. Even if she had lost the baby, she was beyond blessed to have these people in her life. Her heart felt full despite the emptiness inside of her.

"Wait, I thought..." Taryn turned to Tiana, suddenly remembering.

"Shhh...when your brother called, we changed our flights so we could come up earlier," Tiana interjected.

"I love you, guys." She smiled through her sobs as she hugged her mom, her dad coming up from behind and squeezing his little girl. "Um, could I talk to Derek alone for a second? Please?" Taryn asked.

"Of course, we'll be right outside," Nathan said as they all headed out of the room, closing the door behind them.

Before Taryn could say anything, Derek smashed his mouth onto hers hungrily, wrapping his arms around her waist and pulling her up to him. He maneuvered them so she was cradled in his lap as he sat with her on the bed. Taryn melted into his arms, letting whatever tears she had left pour out from her body.

"I love you," Derek said, pulling back and looking her in the eyes. "This baby or the next or no baby at all. *I love you, Taryn*. I'm here for you. Please let me be here for you," he emphasized, cupping her cheek in his hand, his own eyes full of tears.

"I'm so sorry, Derek. I know how happy you were," Taryn said between sobs. "I'm so sorry."

"Shhh. Like your mom said, you have nothing to apologize for. All I need is *you*. Any baby on top of that is just a bonus person to have our love overflow onto." Derek sighed. "We'll get through this together, and it'll just make us better parents when we are blessed with another baby. It'll make us appreciate and love them that much more."

"Us? Another baby?" Taryn could barely get the words past her lips. "Have you been thinking about that?"

"I told you, Taryn, I'm not going anywhere. You're it for me, okay? And I will spend every day proving that to you until I take my last breath." Derek began to sob himself.

Overcome by emotion, Taryn buried her face into his chest and cried, wrapping her arms around his waist and squeezing him to her as if trying to meld their bodies into one. Derek wrapped his arms around her neck and kissed the top of her head. He wished with all his might that he could take this pain from her, but with Taryn in his arms, he knew he would be the strength to get both of them through this loss. Together, they would be okay. Together, they could find happiness again.

"I love you," he said into her hair.

"I love you too, Derek," Taryn finally uttered the words she never thought she'd ever say aloud to another man. His heartbeat quickened in his chest, pounding against his peck as she rested her head on it.

"I love you. I love you. I love you," Derek whispered over and over again as he rocked her back and forth, showering her face with kisses. In this moment, Taryn knew she would be okay.

23

Derek

Derek did not leave Taryn's side, even refusing her parents' offer to stay with her so he could go home to shower and rest. After they were done filming for the day, his friends came to visit, Annie bringing some soup dumplings for Taryn to make her feel better. Taryn put on a brave face, smiled, and even held conversation with them. Derek told her she didn't need to see anyone if she didn't want to, but she insisted, wanting to show her gratefulness for their support. Taryn had fallen asleep, exhausted from the day once everyone left. Sitting in the chair next to her, Derek refused to release her hand and watched her sleep.

Just before midnight, strange noises slipped from her lips. He sat up startled and looked at her. She was still fast asleep. Watching her carefully, the noises came again. This time, they were clear. She was crying in her sleep, tears pushing their way past her clenched eyelids, rolling down her cheeks. Derek's heart crumbled, and he felt utterly helpless just sitting there. He wished he could take all the pain from her and wanted to just squeeze her to his chest, protecting her from the world. Even if she was putting on a brave face for everyone else, it was clear to him now that she was silently suffering more than he could imagine on the inside. Suddenly, she sat up wide awake, panting.

"Are you okay?" Derek whispered, rubbing her arm.

"Yes…no." She broke down.

"Shhh. It's okay," Derek said as he got up and sat on the edge of her bed, squeezing next to her leg as he placed his hands gently, one on each side of her body.

"I saw her," Taryn's voice broke as she drew sad eyes up to Derek.

"Who? Who did you see?" Derek asked, confused.

"The baby." She sobbed on a hushed sigh. "She was little already, walking. Then in a flash, it's like time rewound. I saw her getting smaller and smaller until she disappeared completely. I tried to hold her in my arms, protect her, keep her there, but there was nothing I could do to stop her from vanishing before my eyes."

Derek had no idea how to respond. Taryn saw their baby growing up and then suddenly torn away from her. The pain in his heart thinking about what she must have felt, even in her dream, was unbearable.

"Taryn." He sighed as he laid next to her and pulled her into his side. "I'm sorry I can't give that to you right now, but I promise when we do have a little one, it will bring greater joy than any dream, and it won't be ripped away."

Taryn looked up at him with her tear-filled eyes.

"Thank you for being here." She sighed.

"I wouldn't be anywhere else." He smiled, wiping a tear from her cheek. "I told you, I'm not going anywhere."

On a grateful sigh, Taryn buried her face into his chest, wrapping her arms around his waist and squeezing him to her with her fragile arms. Holding her there, he knew they would get through this together. He would make sure they got through this if it was the last thing he ever did.

24

Taryn

It had been a little over two weeks since her stint in the ER and losing the baby. The dean wanted her to just finish the rest of the course online, but Taryn refused coming to a two-week-off compromise. Derek had stayed with her all weekend, bringing her with him to set, having her rest in his trailer or sitting and watching him film when he had to work. Even if doctors said not to push herself, she was appreciative of having something to do instead of staying at the apartment moping around all day in her own misery. She enjoyed the distraction. Today though, she had her classes to teach. It was the Thursday before the last week of the summer courses, and she wasn't going to miss one final chance to help her students on their projects. They needed her right now and vice versa.

"Are you sure you feel up to teaching today?" Lewis asked as they pulled into the university parking lot.

"No, but it's a good distraction. I have to be in my happy place right now, Lew." Taryn smiled.

As they entered the classroom, students slowly began to trickle in behind them, all with concern on their faces as Taryn greeted them with a smile. Since canceling classes the last two weeks, rumors circled about what happened.

"Hey, Ms. Ti, are you okay?" Sylvia asked.

"No, but I will be. Time heals all wounds or at least teaches you how to live with them on your own terms." Taryn smiled before turning her attention to the whole class. "I apologize for my absence so close to the end of the course. I had something come up. But we'll begin the mock-class projects immediately, cutting the time and scenarios down next week. And as long as you participate, I have been given the green light to use that as your final grade, so no reflection paper!"

Without a hitch, her students followed the instructions, ecstatically practicing and timing themselves. Before she knew it, the day was done, and Lewis was taking her back to the apartment. The entire day at the university was a blur. Taryn went through the motions and got lost in teaching, giving her a much-needed escape. Back at the apartment, Lewis put her things on the kitchen table and took some leftovers out of the fridge to microwave.

"You sure you're okay?" Lewis asked, the humming of the microwave echoing in the space behind him.

"I'll be fine, go. You still have a long drive to get back home." Taryn smiled.

"All right. I texted Derek, and he knows that you are at home, and Nathan said he'd be home soon," he replied with a hug. "And eat!" He motioned to the microwave.

"I promise." Taryn sighed. Lewis hesitated in the doorway, unsure if he should leave. "I'll be fine, Lewie. My parents should be back from their massage soon too."

On a nod, Lewis closed the door behind him, and Taryn was all alone. She sighed as she took the food out of the microwave, forcing herself to eat something before she passed out and drew herself a bath. Soaking in the water, the bubbles created a cushion of calm around her. The warmth of the water soothed her thirsty skin. Taryn closed her eyes as she tried to relax.

"How was your classes?" Derek's deep, smooth voice melted her insides like butter, sending a tingling sensation down her spine.

"Hey. You're done early?" Taryn smiled, turning to find him in the doorway. Ever since they came back to San Francisco, she seemed to be connected to his ninja-like ways, with them no longer startling her like before.

"Yeah, we got the shots we needed within a few takes. I just wanted to come home to you already," he said, sitting on the ledge of the tub.

"You could've taken your time." She smiled. "I'm okay. Everyone should be home within the hour."

"Yes, but I told them I was going to take you out tonight." He smiled gently. "So let's get you out of that tub, and I've got a surprise for you, okay?" Derek leaned down and kissed her gently on the head before heading back into her bedroom.

Taryn finished washing up and dried herself off, wrapping the towel around her body. Pulling the plug on the tub, the water and bubbles drained away, taking some of the anguish she felt with it. Checking her phone, she had a text message from her mom.

Have fun with Derek. Try to smile and be open-minded, okay? We're going with out to dinner with Nathan and Sienna. We'll see you when you get back in a few days. Love you! (Mom)

When I get back? In a few days? Taryn thought to herself, confused. She thought he was just taking her out to a nice dinner or something. What could he have planned for her that wouldn't bring her back for a few days? Didn't he have to film as well? As she walked into the room, Derek had already packed her small duffel bag with clothes. He smiled at her nonchalantly as she approached her bed with cautious eyes.

"So I got this weird text from my mom? Where are you taking me that I won't be back for a few days?" Taryn asked with a nervous smile.

"It's a surprise," he said, stepping in front of her, taking her waist into his arms. "Just trust me, please."

"Okay. I guess I have no choice, huh?" She sighed.

"Come on, we need to get going. Plane leaves in an hour," he said, taking her hands and kissing her on the forehead.

"Wait...plane?" Taryn repeated with a nervous chuckle.

"Yes, plane. It leaves in hour," he said, smiling. "But one hour doesn't give us too much time. So get ready. It'll take us at least thirty minutes, depending on traffic, to get to the airport."

"Okay." She sighed with a smile, grabbing a few more things and shoving it into the duffel bag before throwing her favorite black tracksuit on with a pair of Nike sneakers. Within minutes, she was ready with her purse, phone, and duffel in hand. Derek grabbed the bag from her, taking her hand in his, and they were out the door.

*****

At the airport, she was greeted warmly by his castmates. Everyone had a small to-go bag and were smiling with excitement as they walked into the terminal. His producers were there, and some of the film crew as well. Taryn followed behind Derek slowly, feeling uneasy about crashing a work trip or getting him in trouble for having tagged along.

"I'm going on a work trip with you?" Taryn whispered.

"Something like that." Derek smiled.

"Taryn!" Ananya exclaimed. "Glad you came!"

"Thanks, but I'm not sure where we're going to?" Taryn said hesitantly.

"Girl! We have to film some stuff on-site down Orange County, so we talked Mindy into letting us make a weekend out of it." Ananya smiled wittily. "No sense paying all this money to fly us down for one day, right?"

"Right," Mindy said from a chair in the terminal, rolling her eyes behind Ananya.

"And since we'd only be filming tomorrow morning to early afternoon, I have something special planned for us tonight," Derek said, leaning down and whispering into Taryn's ear from behind.

The warmth of his voice kissed her neck, sending shivers down her spine that ignited that fire in her tummy, the throbbing wetness between her legs awakening. Derek slid his arms around her waist and pulled her into his chest. His chiseled abs firm against her back, his semi-erect cock pressing into her behind.

"Derek." She sighed, trying to control herself. "I…"

"If you're not ready, it's okay, baby. We can start trying again whenever you want to. I love you," he whispered into her hair with a kiss, feeling the apprehension of her recent ordeal, making the thought of sex a little too intense for her to handle just yet.

"Thank you." Taryn smiled, letting out a sigh of relief.

Just as Derek had said, within the hour, they all boarded the plane and were off to Orange County. The plan was to fly into LAX and take a big tour bus down to their hotel near the location they'd be filming at. Taryn tried to relax in the chair as they went. The plane ride was smooth and quick, with everything that had to get done moving in a mechanical fashion, Taryn simply being a bystander watching and following Derek.

It was craziness from the minute they landed. But once they were settled into their hotel, Taryn finally had a chance to breathe and take in the last few hours. Waking up that morning, she would never have thought that after her first day back in the classroom, after being out for two weeks, that she would be on a plane taking a trip a few hours later.

"Since we'll be filming almost all day tomorrow, Em and Reggie going to come down to spend the day with you while I'm on set if that's okay," Derek said as he sat next to her on the bed.

"I don't need babysitters, D." Taryn sighed.

"I know, but they want to see you, and I figured it'd be a lot more fun than just sitting on set, doing nothing all day," Derek reasoned.

"If you insist. I promise I'll just go with it." She smiled.

"Thank you," Derek said, leaning over and kissing her on the forehead. "Now let's go get showered and get you ready for my surprise."

"This trip wasn't the surprise?" Taryn scoffed nervously. "Shouldn't you go with everyone else? To do cast bonding tonight or whatever?"

"No, it wasn't the surprise, and I'll be spending majority of the day with them tomorrow so they can spare me for tonight." Derek winked. "Now let's hurry it up, beautiful. We don't want to be late."

After a quick shower and throwing a touch of makeup on, she was almost ready. It was just after 11:00 p.m., and she still couldn't figure out where he was taking her or what would be open this late. Taryn was wearing a black satin spaghetti strap dress that Derek had surprised her with when she got out of the shower. It was just her size, and he had paired it perfectly with silver strappy sandals he had also gifted her with. He was dressed in black slacks and a matching black button-up shirt, with a silver tie hanging from his neck. His brown curls were combed over, and a white gold watch adorned his wrist.

"You got us matching clothes?" She smiled as she put on the dress over a black lace thong and strapless bra.

"Actually, Sienna and Nathan helped to pick everything out." Derek sighed. "Although I'm regretting that now."

"Why? Is it too dressy for whatever you have planned?" Taryn was worried and felt self-conscious all of a sudden. "I can change into some jeans."

"No, it's not the clothes or where we're going." He blushed, swallowing hard as he stared at her. "You just look like perfection already without anything on."

"We can just stay here if you want?" Taryn said. "I told you, I don't need fancy surprises."

"Yes, and, yes, but this one is special. Lying in bed with you can wait," Derek replied, standing in front of her, wrapping his arms around her waist, and thrusting his hips forward. Leaning down and kissing her on the cheek, he whispered, "Besides, like I said, only when you're ready again. No matter how much I want to be with you, you're worth the wait."

Derek suddenly pulled out a black silk handkerchief from his pocket, dragging it slowly across the exposed skin on her back, making Taryn's breath catch.

"What is that for?" she asked nervously.

"You'll see." He smiled. "Come on, let's go."

In the elevator, Derek used the handkerchief to blindfold her eyes just as the doors closed, saying he didn't want her to see anything just yet. When they reached the bottom floor, the elevator bell rang, and with his warm hands on her shoulders, he guided her out of the elevator. Her heels clicked on the hard tile of the lobby as she blindly allowed Derek to take the lead, guiding her with one hand on the small of her back. Taryn hated that she didn't have control over what was happening, but instead of letting it drive her crazy, she forced herself to go with the flow and to put her trust in Derek.

25

Derek

Taryn looked beautiful in the dress Sienna had picked out for her. Everything tonight had to be perfect, and Derek couldn't risk messing it up. His heart thumped in his chest as they stepped off the elevator, and he began to guide her toward the doors. Outside of their hotel, in the roundabout area, leading up to the lobby entrance, the horse-drawn carriage he ordered was waiting for them. Being so near to Disneyland, he was able to reserve their exact replica of the famous white-and-silver pumpkin carriage from Cinderella. The carriage was round with silver bars shaping its sphere, each wrapped in thousands of twinkling white lights that mirrored the stars in the sky. Two gigantic, pure-white Clydesdale horses were harnessed to the front, a driver held the silver reins in a fancy costume, sitting atop a large bench to guide them, and another held the door to the carriage open as he waited for Derek and Taryn to approach.

"You ready?" Derek whispered into her ear as he stopped her just yards away from the carriage, just far enough for her to get the entire scene in view. She nodded yes without a word. Derek untied the blindfold and let it fall to her side as she let out a little gasp at the beauty standing in front of her. Her eyes scanned every inch of the carriage with wide eyes and in complete awe as she took it all in.

"Derek!" she exclaimed excitedly. "What? How? I don't even know what to say!" she stuttered as she took a deep breath, rendered utterly speechless.

"Do you like it?" he asked as he wrapped his arms around her waist and pulled her into his body. Resting his chin on her shoulder, he continued, "My dad sold homes to some pretty big-timers at Disney, managers, park executives, and whatnot. So he was able to help me pull a few strings to arrange this for tonight."

"I love it." She sighed as she turned in his arms to face him. Her eyes began to glass over with tears of joy. "You did this all for me?"

"I'd do anything for you." He leaned down and kissed her forehead. If she thought this was something, then he couldn't wait to see her reaction to what he had in store for her the rest of the evening. "Come on, they're going to take us to dinner."

She wrapped her hand around the bend in his arm as he led her to the carriage. With a nod, the assistant held the door open as Derek helped her in. The white seat was soft, the pillows smooth to the touch as he climbed in and plopped down next to Taryn. She was glowing with joy as the twinkling of the carriage lights and stars kissed her face. She was gorgeous, and Derek felt like the luckiest man in the world.

The carriage ride was steadier than he had imagined as the horses pulled them along a cobblestone path on the back side of the Disneyland Park, the castle a short distance away, signifying where they were. Knowing Taryn needed to find happiness after losing the baby, Derek's father had helped him arrange it so they could relish in moments of privacy together, rekindling that spark they had before tragedy rocked their lives. As the carriage pulled to a stop, the same assistant opened the door for Derek to get out. He took Taryn's hand and helped her down the two steps. Before leaving, the driver gave her two apples, one to give to each of the horses as a "thank you" which Taryn did with absolute glee.

"Horses are my favorite animal, you know." She smiled to Derek as she held her hand flat, the apple on top for the horse to eat. Taryn giggled as the horse's lips ticked her palm, and the apple disappeared.

Taryn's face looked like a little kid trying to take in everything she possibly could as they went. After walking down a path hidden by bushes, a large wooden gate came into view. As they approached, a Disneyland cast member smiled at them, pushing it open and letting them into the park right next to the Haunted Mansion ride.

"Wait, what?" She laughed excitedly. "This is my…"

"Favorite ride?" Derek finished for her. "I know. I asked Nathan. Now come on, we only got a small window for this," he said, taking her hand and leading her toward the ride.

"Small window for what?" She smiled.

"To have the ride all to ourselves." He winked.

Her eyes grew wide in amazement and excitement as she bit down on her lip and followed him. He couldn't help but laugh to himself as he guided her to the entrance of the ride. His heart jumped to see her so happy, and he thought to himself how he could truly live every day, happy like this, just being able to see her smile.

As they walked up the stone steps and into a large empty room, the walls started to rise as they were transported underground into darkness. Music played, and picture frames with dancing, talking portraits were adorned on the walls around them. Once they reached the bottom, a door opened off to the side, taking them down a long corridor with red velvet carpet and more *ghostly* portraits lining the hallway.

"So why do you like this ride?" Derek asked as their eyes adjusted to the darkness.

"It's all in the detailing. We'd come during the holidays, and the details they put are mind-blowing. You have to ride it at least five times to even notice everything. And the doom buggies you ride in are pretty cool too." She smiled as they approached a large black sphere.

Stepping onto a moving walkway, one of the doom-buggy seats stopped in front of them, the bar dropping to allow them to sit. Swiftly, they maneuvered their bodies just in time to plop down in the giant black shell.

"This is pretty cozy." Derek sighed, draping his arm around her shoulder. Taryn scooted closer, resting her arm over his lap as she leaned into his chest.

The ride began, and they were twirled around to face different walls as the doom buggy moved them through the house. Taryn pointed out so many details and a few hidden Mickeys that Derek never noticed before. It blew his mind just like she said it would, and he could barely keep up with taking everything in. She loved it all, and he loved having her next to him to share the moment with.

"How do you know this ride so well?" he questioned, knowing she lived in Hawai'i her entire life without any theme parks of their own back home.

"It was always one of my favorite movies growing up and one of the rides I would constantly want to go on when we would come up for vacations as a family." She sighed. "We'd come once a year until Nathan was in high school."

"What happened after that? Why didn't you guys keep coming?" Derek wondered.

"Well, I was working a lot to put myself through college, and Nathan started coming up with his high school. One of his classes used to do all these competitions on the mainland, and they'd always go to Disneyland, so we'd do staycations instead over school breaks," she explained. "Plus, Grandma's dementia started getting really bad, and it was just too difficult to leave her for long periods of time. It just got harder to do family trips the older we got."

Derek was learning more and more about her, and she seemed to get more wonderful with each detail she shared. As the ride came to an end, they hopped off and walked up another moving walkway until they were at the exit at the back of the mansion.

"So what's next?" She smiled. "I hate surprises, but this is pretty amazing so far."

"Well, you're just going to have to see," he said, offering his elbow for her to take.

They took a short walk through the park until they reached the castle. The park had a different magic to it, nearly empty as it was about to close to the public for the day. A smile beamed across

Taryn's face as she stared at the thousands of lights glittering the castle. On the ground just at the entrance, before you walk through the castle, was a large blanket adorned with little pillows and rose petals scattered about. A large picnic basket lay off to the side.

"You planned me a picnic?" She smiled, tears filing her eyes. "I've never been on a picnic."

"Really?" Derek was surprised. "I figured Hawai'i would be the perfect place to picnic, like at the beach or whatever. The weather is almost always picnic perfect, right?"

"I'm serious!" Taryn giggled. "Back home, when we say that we're going to picnic at the beach, it's more of just hanging out at the beach with snacks shoved in a cooler and everyone sprawled out on their own towels."

"Oh." Derek nodded. "Well, welcome to your first picnic, my lady, have a seat. I'll get the food out."

As Taryn sat down, Derek dug in the basket, pulling out different black containers, with food he had ordered from Steakhouse 55 at the Disneyland hotel. There were New York steaks, already precut, mashed potatoes, Caesar salad, tomato bisque soup, and their famous jumbo lump crab cakes. He opened the containers and set them about between Taryn and himself.

"This all looks and smells delicious," she said as Derek handed her a fork.

"Eat up!" He smiled. "Steakhouse 55 is one of the restaurants we'd always go to for birthdays in our family. I'd say they have the best food you'll find in Orange County."

Putting piece of steak on her fork, scooping up some mashed potatoes behind it, Taryn chewed deliciously. Her eyes closed, and a little moan slipped past her lips. Derek couldn't help but swallow hard just watching her, the fire in his groin instantly igniting at the sounds slipping from her lips as she ate.

"This is so good!" She sighed contently.

"I'm glad you like it, Ti," he replied, with his heart feeling as full as his stomach was becoming. "Here, try some of their crab cakes. It's amazing." Derek broke off a piece on his fork and held it out for her to bite.

"You're feeding me now?" She laughed as she took his fork between her teeth on a smile.

"I was trying to be cute," he said sarcastically. "Did it work?"

"Yes, it did." Taryn giggled as she covered her mouth with her hand, hiding her face as she chewed. "But wow, this is really good."

"Wait until dessert," Derek said, turning back to the basket and pulling out two more black containers.

"What are those?" she asked, eyes wide with excitement. "I love desserts. I could literally make a meal just eating appetizers and desserts."

"First, we have their twenty-four-layer chocolate cake. It's very decadent, but it's their signature dessert, so I figured I'd get it for you to try," Derek answered, opening the lid on the first container. Popping open the second, he continued, "And this, is their vanilla bean caramel crème brûlée. Nathan said your favorite dessert is crème brûlée, so I had to get you theirs just in case the cake wasn't your cup of tea."

"Thank you, Derek. All of this…it's beyond thoughtful and generous." Taryn sighed. "I don't even know what to say at this point. I'm totally blown away."

"I'm glad you're enjoying it." He smiled. "But, Ti, you don't have to say anything. You deserve to be treated like a queen and taken care of. I love you."

"I love you too, Derek," her voice cracked as tears started to glass her eyes over. "I'm sorry I was pushing you away before. I just didn't want to get hurt again. But…"

"Taryn, you don't need to explain yourself. With everything you've gone through, your actions were more than justified, and you handled yourself with a level of poise that most people wouldn't be able to," Derek interrupted.

"Derek, please let me finish." She sighed with a smile, pausing for him to notion her to continue. "Before I got pregnant, I honestly felt like I had nothing left in this world already. Everyone I cared about had someone to be with or take care of them. It just felt like I was constantly messing everything up. Then when we got pregnant, I was ecstatic. But when lost the baby, I felt like it was the world telling me I don't deserve to be happy, that my job is to make other people happy, not myself. That if I tried to be happy, I would only get hurt again. But I'm slowly realizing that everything happens for a reason. I don't think we would be as close as we are now with the world slamming us in each other's lives so rapidly if we didn't go through that together. And I appreciate you beyond words for sticking by my side through it. If I'm being honest, I couldn't have done it without you, Derek. I'm really grateful that it's you that my heart chose to open up to."

Taryn had summed up his feelings in her own words. How she felt for him was exactly how he felt for her. From the moment they met, he was drawn to her, and it flipped his world upside down. He realized from that first time she left, he wouldn't be able to do life without her by his side, and that belief solidified itself with Lexie's murder.

Unable to control his emotions anymore and having no words to explain his feelings, he pushed the food to the side, leaning forward to kiss her tenderly. They each needed someone in their lives to fix them, and in each other, they had finally become whole again. They were each other's missing pieces, what each other needed to finally heal and move on with their lives.

"I love you, Taryn," Derek said through their kiss, his forehead resting on hers, their noses touching, and their lips mere millimeters apart.

"I love you too, Derek." She smiled before kissing him back. Her lips tasted delicious, and the warmth of her mouth sent blood rushing to his cock.

"Come on. I got one more surprise for you," Derek added, trying to calm himself down.

"There's more? What more could you have under your sleeves? This is already too much." Taryn chuckled.

"You'll see," he said, peeling himself away from her and sitting up. Derek covered all the food as Taryn placed the basket to the side. "We just need to take the food and the basket with us. My dad's friend will come for the rest."

"You sure? I can clean up," she said, already picking up each individual rose petal by hand.

"I'm sure, baby. Just stack these nicely in the basket as I pass them to you if you want to help, okay?" Derek smiled, trying to reason with her compulsive cleaning.

"Okay." She sighed as she patiently waited for him to pass her the food containers. Placing them neatly in the basket, she smiled at her work, causing Derek to giggle to himself.

"What?" She sighed, noticing him watching her as she organized the basket.

"Nothing, you're just cute," he said as he closed the basket, took it in one hand, and offered her his other. "You ready?"

"With you by my side? I am ready for anything." Taryn smiled as she interwove her fingers with his, and they headed down Main Street toward the Disneyland exit.

26

Taryn

"You got us access to California Adventure too?" Taryn exclaimed in shock as another worker stood by the park entrance, opposite of Disneyland, and let them in thorough a side gate with a simple nod from Derek.

"Yes." He laughed. "I told you, I had something special planned."

"The trip down here alone was special. All of this is above and beyond, Derek. You really didn't need to," Taryn argued.

"Hush, it's fine. I wanted to spoil you a little, so stop arguing and just let me do it, okay? Please?" Derek pleaded with puppy-dog eyes.

"This is the last part of the surprise?" Taryn said hesitantly.

"Yes," he replied.

"Promise? I already feel bad, Derek. This is way too much." She sighed.

"I promise." Derek smiled, kissing her on the forehead. "Don't feel bad, please. Stop thinking for once and just enjoy yourself. You deserve it and more."

"Fine." She sighed heavily.

"Okay." He smiled, pulling her through the park, past the waterfall at the backside of Grizzly River Run until they were at the entrance to the Pixar Pier. Squeezing her hand, they walked over the bridge. The park seeming peaceful as if it were sleeping without the normal hustle and bustle of crowds. Walking alongside the pier, they passed the Incredicoaster and the Toy Story Midway Mania rides until they came to Mickey's Fun Wheel, a large Ferris wheel that towered over the man-made lagoon. The lights to the Ferris wheel suddenly came on as they walked toward the entrance to the ride.

"The Ferris wheel?" She smiled as she wrapped her arms around his in excitement.

"Yes, the Ferris wheel. I figured it's like the most 'romantic' ride at carnivals, right? And it's pretty mellow so you can rest and digest the food. I thought it'd be the perfect way to end our night," Derek replied as a worker opened the door to one of the stationary gondolas, and they stepped in. Placing the picnic basket on one of the benches, he settled in next to her on the other.

"Boss said to let you run on a loop for fifteen minutes, so the ride will just keep going. Text him if you want to stop early. Have fun, you two," the worker said, closing the door and locking it before turning to leave.

The lights of the Ferris wheel dimmed as it started moving in circles. The only light that could be seen was that of the large Mickey Mouse head in the center. Darkness surrounded them while their gondola rose and fell as the wheel took them around, continuously lifting them upward to the sky. The lights of the city in the distance and the rest of the park looked tiny, scattered across the ground. The purples and reds of the Mickey lights kissed Taryn's face, setting it aglow.

"This night is just too perfect, Derek. I can't thank you enough," she said, scooting into his side. He draped his arm around her as he squeezed her to him.

"You don't have to thank me. Just seeing you happy is thanks enough." Derek tilted her head up to him as his lips tenderly found hers, sucking the air from her lungs. "I love you, Taryn."

"I love you, Derek," Taryn said with a happy sigh, her heart fuller than she could ever imagine.

27

Derek

Everything went perfectly as they got back to the hotel. His plan had been a success, and happiness was seeping from every inch of Taryn's being. As he watched her walk in front of him, Derek was beyond yearning for Taryn, his desire thick with a needing to lose himself inside of her. But he knew he couldn't push it, and he would never want to rush things with her after what she had been through. Having their physical connection would come again when she was ready, and he was willing to wait for her until then. As the elevator doors shut behind them, Taryn suddenly pushed him up against the wall and crashed her mouth onto his, making his knees buckle.

"You're going to get it once I get you behind closed doors," she heaved, her voice drenched in desire as the elevator made its slow journey up to their floor.

"We're behind closed doors already," he teased.

"Don't tempt me," Taryn replied seductively.

As the elevator dinged, signifying they were at their destination, Taryn walked backward down the hallway sexily, watching Derek follow her with hungry eyes until her back was pressed up against the door to their room. His mouth crashed on hers hungrily as he used one hand to open the door with the key card, causing them both to stumble backward. Taryn's hands shot up to Derek's neck as their tongues danced.

Closing the door behind him, Derek reached back and flipped the extra lock latch over, refusing to break their kiss. Dropping the food basket on the ground, he immediately lifted Taryn up to his body, her legs wrapping instinctively around his waist as her hands rushed to yank off his tie, throwing it to the ground. As he neared the chair, he placed her on her feet gently while she made quick work of removing his shirt and tossing it aside.

"I missed this." She sighed with lust-filled eyes as her hands landed on his shoulder muscles before she dragged her fingertips down his chest and rested on his abs, pushing him to sit in a chair in the corner of the room.

Tucking a knee next to his thighs, Taryn straddled him, their tongues continued to dance. Grabbing the seam of her dress, he lifted it over her head and discarded it to the floor. Running his hands up the smooth skin on her back, he found the hook to her bra and undid it, exposing her.

"Are you sure, baby?" Derek pulled back suddenly, wanting to make sure Taryn was ready and not just doing this because she was caught in the moment after a perfect evening together.

"Yes." Taryn smiled. "I'm positive."

"As you wish," he said, gripping her bottom and standing with her, the muscles on his arms flexing as he squeezed her to him.

Leaning down, he placed her gently on the bed, kissing her lips. Slowly, he trailed kisses down her body, his lips trailing kisses down the center of her chest and across her tummy. Taryn lifted her hips so he could finish removing her clothing, tossing her panties to the ground. He stood above her for a second, admiring her beauty as she lay on the bed completely exposed, her head tilted to the side as her nipples hardened under his stare. She watched him intently as he unbuckled his belt and pants; pushing them down with his boxers, he discarded them to the floor. Taking his length in his hand, Derek knelt down, wedging himself between Taryn's legs as he slowly worked his way upward toward her.

"I'm going to take you slow," Derek whispered into her ear as he rained gentle kisses on her neck and collarbone, his length caressing the soft skin of her inner thigh.

Dipping his hips slowly, he began to pulse toward her as his tip met her entrance, already wet and waiting for him. As he grinded forward deliciously, he could feel every inch of her warm skin wrap around him as he found himself in her depths, causing a moan to escape past Taryn's lips. Slowly, his hips rose as her muscles fought to hold him inside of her.

"Derek." She panted, biting down on her bottom lip, gripping his forearms as they tensed around her face.

Taryn's eyes were clenched shut, and sweat already started forming on his chest, making her glisten every time he rubbed against her body. Dipping down again, he pushed as far into her as he could possibly go, stealing all breath from Taryn's lungs as she gasped for air. Holding himself there, he braced an arm on either side of her head, his biceps bulging and framing her face.

"You okay, baby?" He panted as he held himself there, brushing her hair from her forehead.

Nodding, Taryn looked up at him as he kissed her forehead before dipping his hips back down, pulsing his hips into her as he entered her over and over again. The short, quick bursts of friction caused him to twitch inside of her. He could feel her start clenching around him as her legs shot up and wrapped around his waist, her hands gripping frantically at the sheets around her. She was almost there.

"Come on, baby," he said, brushing another stray strand of hair from her face, watching her as her eyes rolled back on a moan.

"Don't stop." She panted.

"Never baby," he said, kissing her on a final dip of his hips, their releases taking over as their bodies clenched onto one another. Derek collapsed on top of her as their hands continued to explore each other, guiding each other down from their climaxes. As they lay there tangled in each other catching their breath, Derek rolled over and pulled her into his body as she smiled against his chest.

"I love you." Taryn sighed as she relaxed into him.

"I love you too." He smiled as he held her in his arms, both of them refusing to be torn from that moment.

28

Taryn

After the whirlwind of a night, Taryn and Derek fell asleep in each other's arms with glee, their naked bodies intertwined, his hard chest pressing up against her back. The warmth of Derek next to her gave her unsurpassed comfort that she could never have imagined she would have found again. She was whole again, closer than ever before to Derek, with him being the pieces that fixed what was broken inside of her for so long.

Blinking her eyes to adjust to the darkness of their room, she sighed happily as she snuggled in closer to him, taking a moment to listen to his breathing and feel his heart beat against her. Looking over to the alarm clock on the hotel nightstand, it was just before 6:00 a.m., and the sun had barely risen, but Taryn was wide awake. She had a little more than an hour left with him until Derek had to report to the set fifteen minutes away. Taryn turned in his arms to face him, prompting his arms to instinctively pull her closer and squeeze her onto his chest.

"No," he groaned. "Five more minutes." Derek curled his large body up into her side and shoved his face in her neck as if trying to hide from the world.

"Okay," Taryn whispered into his ear, crooning her neck to kiss him on the cheek.

She ran her hands down his chest, exploring his body, resting them on his abs, feeling the tensing of his stomach muscles with every breath he took. Even when relaxed, they were rock-solid. Tracing his V-cut with her index fingers, she slowly ran her palms over his hips until they found the dip in his back. She began to caress his soft skin, rubbing her fingers up and down the length of his lower back muscles as she sighed to herself at the thought of how lucky she was to have such a strong man, physically and emotionally, in her life. She would not have gotten through these past few months without him.

"Good morning, beautiful," Derek's raspy voice pulled her from her thoughts.

"Hey, handsome." She smiled as she pushed a strand of hair from his forehead and kissed it.

"You make me want to stay here and hide from the rest of the world forever." Derek sighed as he crawled onto her, wrapping himself around her body like a spider monkey.

"You have to though. Your people have been so understanding about me. You can't let them down, okay?" she reasoned. "Film today, and then tomorrow, we can spend the day together with all of your friends."

"Promise?" he asked jokingly as if he were a little child.

"I promise." She smiled as he leaned down and kissed her nose. "I love you, Derek."

"I love you, Ti." He smiled back as he placed a gentle kiss on her tummy. "Let's get washed up. I don't want to send you off to have lunch with Emma smelling like a night's worth of sex." Derek winked.

"She wouldn't know what that smells like unless she's been there with Reggie," Taryn joked, making Derek's face twist in disgust.

"Geez. Thanks a lot, Ti." He laughed. "I really needed that image in my head of my baby sister."

"Sorry." She laughed as she stepped into the shower with him. "You asked for it."

"Yeah…sure, I did." He laughed, wrapping his arms around her waist as he scrubbed her down with soap and a wash cloth.

Between play-fighting to wash one another and little romantic kisses here and there, the two of them were pruned by the time they got out of the shower. As Taryn got dried off, Derek got ready to head to set. He had a fresh comforter delivered to the room so she could go back to sleep.

"I'll see you tonight, okay?" he said. Taryn sat up and moved to sit on the edge of the bed as he leaned down and kissed her tenderly.

"Okay. Don't be too long though." She winked as he turned to leave. "Break a leg."

As he closed the door behind him, Taryn's heart soared with hope and happiness. Maybe, everything would be okay after all.

29

Derek

Stepping onto set, Derek's heart felt light, and he was the happiest he had been in a long time. Everything had gone perfectly with Taryn, and he was excited to see how the summer would end now that they seemed to be back on good terms. Despite running off just a few hours of sleep, he felt energized and renewed somehow.

"Someone had a good night," Jared teased as he entered the hair-and-makeup trailer.

"Yes, I did. How was dinner last night with everyone else?" Derek asked.

"It went well. Although I'm sure our night was nowhere as interesting as yours," he replied, sitting next to Derek.

"It was perfect." Derek smiled on a sigh.

"That's it? That's all the details you're giving?" Ben interjected as he came up on the opposite side of Derek, leaning against the counter to face him. "Come on, give us something, bro!"

"The food was good, and she was ecstatic about getting to go on the rides." Derek chuckled.

"I'm sure she was," Ben said teasingly on raised eyebrows. "I bet you were her favorite ride."

"Stop!" Derek scolded. "It wasn't like that."

"Uh-huh. Sure, D. We could see your sex smile from a mile away," Ben argued.

"Don't listen to him, D. We're glad your night went well," Jared reasoned.

"Well, let's get out there. They're going to start shooting soon." Derek sighed.

Standing up, the three of them exited the trailer and headed to set. Today, they were filming the state water polo championship match for the season finale episode. Their characters were all supposed to be on the underdog team that challenges the defending champs. During the match, someone from the other team is supposed to get a seizure in the water, and Derek's character is going to be the one to save the day, sacrificing his game-winning shot to save the person's life. It would be a long day in the pool, and he would be pruned by the end of it, but it didn't matter to Derek. All he could think about was getting it done so he could get back to Taryn.

30

Taryn

"Taryn!" Emma's voice echoed through the door on a knock around 10:45 a.m.

Pulling herself up from the bed, Taryn headed over to the door. After Derek had left, she had thrown on some jeans and a tank top before heading down to grab some coffee and a bagel, before Emma and Reggie arrived. This would be the first time seeing them since the graduation.

"Hey!" She smiled as she opened the door. But instead of seeing Reggie with Emma, their oldest sister was there instead. "Good morning, Em," Taryn said uncomfortably. She met her at the graduation, but they never really spoke, and Taryn wasn't sure what their oldest sister knew about her and Derek.

"Ti! I missed you!" Emma said, pulling Taryn into a hug. "This is Janie, our oldest sister," she introduced.

"Hi, it's so nice to meet you, officially." Taryn smiled, holding her hand out for Janie to shake.

Janie reluctantly took Taryn's hand and shook it.

"So you're the one who's got my little brother all fucked up in his emotions, huh?" Janie said coldly as she eyed Taryn from head to toe.

"Ease up, Janie!" Emma scoffed at her sister. "Don't mind her, Ti. She hasn't had her coffee yet this morning."

139

"It's fine," Taryn said softly before turning her attention to Janie. "You don't know me yet, so it's fine if you don't trust me with your brother. I'm an older sister myself, and I'm very reserved with the people my brother chooses to date too. I get it. I just hope I can gain your trust once you do get to know me." Taryn smiled at Janie as she let go of her hand.

"We'll see." Janie sighed, giving Taryn one last hard look. "We should get downstairs though. Our reservations are for eleven."

"Okay." Taryn sighed, tossing her bag over her shoulder. She checked to make sure she had the hotel room key and closed the door behind her as she followed Janie and Emma down the hall.

"Reservations?" Taryn asked Emma.

"Yes, reservations. For brunch?" Janie frowned.

"Since Reggie couldn't make it today, I figured we could have brunch downstairs at Tocca Ferro. It's an amazing Italian restaurant. Then we could go shopping at Fashion Island down at Newport Beach. It's this great mall. You'd love it! They even have a huge Barnes & Noble!" Emma jumped in. Janie just continued to watch Taryn carefully.

"That sounds wonderful." Taryn smiled gratefully. "It's been a while since I've had a shopping day like that."

"Shopping is the perfect way to celebrate with the last week of courses coming up for you too!" Emma said cheerfully. "She's teaching the summer courses at USF for 'fun' like a weirdo. She teaches freshman back home while teaching online college courses during the school year. But instead of taking a break like a normal teacher, she wanted to teach not one but *two* classes this summer!" Emma teased.

"Hard worker, I see," Janie noted. "At least we know you're not with our brother for his money."

"I beg your pardon?" Taryn scoffed, shocked and dumbfounded by Janie's forwardness. Even when she hadn't liked one of Nate's ex-girlfriends, Taryn was never outright rude like that.

"J!" Emma scolded. "Taryn is not like that."

On a heavy sigh, they stepped into the elevator as Janie continued, "I'm just saying. Derek is an actor, just breaking out in his craft, and he comes from money because of dad. It's just a positive sign that she is a hard worker and not a leech like that ex of his." Janie's tone was harsh as she pushed the button for the lobby.

"Janie! Even if Lexie wasn't the best person out there, that's not cool to talk down about her like that. She's dead, remember?" Emma argued.

"That was just her karma. I'm not saying what happened to her was okay or that I'm glad she's dead, but after everything she did to D, how nothing was ever good enough for her? When she should've been appreciative of even the smallest gestures coming from absolute trash? Bottom line, she got what she deserved. It was karma," Janie explained on a scoff before turning angry eyes toward Taryn. She was still clearly upset about how much Lexie had put her brother through, and her protective instincts were flaring. "Let me just say this now before I end up liking you, like Em and D say I will...don't use or hurt my brother. He may fuck up from time to time, but he's too good a person for that. I don't want some small-town girl getting a taste for this 'lifestyle' to fuck him up. He's already been through enough, and he doesn't deserve to get hurt again. Understood?"

"Completely," Taryn agreed confidently, locking eyes with Janie. "I would never do anything to intentionally hurt your brother. And as for the money aspect and 'using' him, I would never. I bust my ass for what I have, and I don't need anyone to take care of me. I'm with your brother because I love him, and after what we've been through together, in such a short period of time, I have a connection with him that goes deeper than anything I could describe. Rich or poor, working or unemployed, healthy or sick, the only way I wouldn't stand by his side is if he doesn't want me to be there."

"What do you mean after 'everything' you two have been through?" Janie questioned with dagger eyes as the elevator dinged, signifying they were in the lobby.

The three of them stepped out from the elevator, and Taryn wasn't sure what Janie was getting at. How could she not know about everything? Didn't Derek go home to LA for a while to be with his family? Panic flashed across Emma's face, shaking her head rapidly at Taryn as she stood behind Janie. Instead of answering Janie, Taryn looked up at the signs on the walls and started walking toward the restaurant with Emma. Suddenly, Taryn was yanked around. Janie had a strong grip on her wrist, holding her in place as her eyes pierced right through all of Taryn's defenses.

"What are you talking about, Taryn?" Janie seethed through clench teeth, her eyes narrowing.

"Uh…" Taryn wasn't sure what to say.

She didn't know what Derek did or didn't share with his older sister or why he didn't let her in to begin with. Was it really Taryn's place to say anything if Derek already chose to keep it a secret?

"Janie," Emma tried to reason, "Derek didn't want to tell you because he didn't want you getting upset or going into big-sister mode. Just calm down. People are starting to stare."

Janie's grip eased on Taryn's wrist as her eyes searched the lobby. Multiple faces were stopping to stare at them.

"We'll talk about this at the table. Walk," Janie instructed as Emma and Taryn followed her toward the entrance of the restaurant.

As they entered, a hostess with golden skin stood and greeted them. The large white marble bar, with a mirrored backsplash, came into view, directly behind it.

"Good morning, welcome to Tocca Ferro. May I get a name, please?" the hostess asked with bright red locks pulled back into a ponytail. Her eyes outlined with heavy black eyeliner and detailed with long lashes that touched her eyebrows. Bright red lips adorned an even brighter smile.

"Hi. We have a reservation for three under the name Bennett." Janie smiled at the hostess with fake sincerity.

"Bennett! My apologies, ma'am. Right this way," the hostess stuttered, quickly grappling with some menus before leading them to a small private room, with floor-to-ceiling glass windows at the back of the restaurant. "Your waiter will be with you immediately." She smiled on a nod, closing the door behind her.

The room was cozy, and despite the large windows, it was quite private as gigantic rose bushes towered over, completely surrounding a small garden space just outside. A crystal chandelier hung from the ceiling, and a small marble bar adorned the far corner of the room. Taryn was in awe with her surroundings.

"You've never had a private room at a restaurant before?" Janie questioned as she poured herself a mimosa.

"Nope." Taryn sighed. "I usually just eat with the general population. I've never had this type of special treatment in a restaurant before."

"Well, when you're in the LA-Hollywood-Anaheim area, you need to get used to it if you're going to date Derek." Janie laughed.

"Because he's an actor? He's still just Derek with me though." Taryn was confused.

"Sit down, honey." Janie sighed. Following instructions, Taryn sat down at the table across of Janie as she continued, "It is partially because Derek is an actor that is slowly getting his name known. However, it's more so because of our dad. Even if he's kept us humble for the most part and forced us to learn how to work hard for our ourselves, his name carries a lot of weight in SoCal."

"He was one of the most prominent real estate agents in the area for over twenty years before he opened up his own company about fifteen years ago. Now, as a broker, he has expanded even more, building his own team of amazing agents and partnerships with local construction companies to flip properties of all sizes. He even has branches for his company in multiple major cities across California," Emma explained. "And for the past ten years, he's been selling properties of all sorts, from multimillion-dollar homes of celebrities and top CEOs to fixer-upper homes that he's flipped with his construction partners. Janie's been doing the marketing for him since she graduated from college, and I'm starting to run and balance the financial end of it. He wants to retire in the next five years, so he's been prepping us to take over from birth."

"Wow. That's beyond impressive. I knew he was a real estate guru. I mean we're renting the summer apartment in San Fran from him. But I didn't know he was that big into it. That's amazing." Taryn was stunned.

"I'm sorry, but now you see now why I'm so hesitant to just accept any new person into our family? Especially after the mess of an ex that Derek had." Janie sighed.

"It's completely understandable. I'm so sorry you have to be on guard like that all the time," Taryn replied.

"It's hard trusting people sometimes, but that's why we're extra careful and try not to 'drop' our name right away if you know what I mean," Emma reasoned. "Like Janie's husband actually worked as one of our dad's top agents straight out of college, and we knew him, trusted him for years before they even started dating."

"The same with Reggie. He was friends with Emma for a long time and went out of his way to take care of her in college, so we knew he was with her for her," Janie added.

"And I'm just a random girl that you guys know nothing about who appeared from Hawai'i out of nowhere." Taryn sighed, realizing why Janie was nervous about her. "And with you guys knowing and trusting Lexie for years only to have her put Derek through all that crap, it's like how are you going to trust a complete stranger with him. I totally get it."

"Exactly." Janie smiled, clearly surprised with Taryn's logical thinking, putting two and two together on her own.

"Like I said, I get it. Money makes it harder to trust someone enough to let them into your family, but even without it, you just want what's best for your loved ones. And that gives you every right to be as reserved as you want to be around someone new." Taryn smiled.

Janie was completely silent, her eyes studying Taryn to see if the sincerity in her voice was real.

"See, I told you you'd like her," Emma said, nudging her sister in the arm.

"We'll see," Janie laughed. "But you are starting on a very good note so far." She tipped her glass to Taryn before taking another sip.

A knock came on the door, and a young waiter with his dark hair combed over appeared in the doorway, with a blond waiter holding a tray of appetizers behind him.

"My apologies for taking a while. We heard you conversing and didn't want to interrupt. We've brought you appetizers to start, complimentary, of course, and some waters. Did you, ladies, get a chance to look over the menus yet?" The dark-haired waiter asked as the blond one placed the appetizer plates down on the table before filling their glasses with water.

"It's not a problem. Give us fifteen minutes, and we'll be ready to order." Janie smiled as she sipped her mimosa.

"Perfect. We'll be back in fifteen minutes. As always, hit the red button next to the light switch if you need anything or have any questions before then," the dark-haired waiter said on a nod as they exited the room.

Turning her attention back to Taryn and Emma, Janie smiled as she downed the rest of her mimosa on a sigh and leaned back in her chair.

"So tell me. What is this 'everything' that you have been through with my brother?" Janie asked suspiciously.

"With all due respect, I'm not sure I should be the one telling you. If Derek didn't, then I don't feel it's my place to share things that he may consider 'private' just yet. I'm sorry if you disagree." Taryn sighed.

"Wow." Janie laughed, sitting upright. "That's not the answer I expected, but I do respect you for that. His ex would've just blabbed to get on my good side, but you...you have integrity, and you respect my brother's privacy over your own ego. You have a sense of loyalty for him. I like that."

"Uh...thank you?" Taryn sighed nervously.

"Derek will tell me when he's ready I guess," Janie said, standing and heading back to the bar. "Why don't you tell me about yourself instead. What's your story, Taryn?"

On a heavy sigh and looking to Emma for support, Taryn began summing up her life, filling each second of those fifteen minutes, with details of things she's been through on her own and what brought her and Derek's paths to cross.

"Again, wow." Janie sighed, crossing her arms.

"Yeah, it's been a rough year." Taryn sighed.

"And none of that included whatever it was that brought you and Derek closer together in these past few months?" Janie seemed confused.

"Nope. Derek, in my life, started a whole different story, and everything we've been through together is for him to share to you when he's ready, like you said." Taryn sighed.

"Well, if you're strong enough to go through all of that, I'm confident you're strong enough to handle our family and take care of my brother. Just again, please don't hurt him." Janie smiled gently.

"I promise. I won't." Taryn smiled back.

31

Derek

It was almost 8:00 p.m., and Derek was exhausted from a long day of filming. Dragging his feet down the hallway, he couldn't wait to get back to the hotel room and see Taryn. He hadn't heard from her all day, so he was hoping that it meant things went well with Emma and Reggie. As he stuck his hotel room key in the slot, he heard girls giggling from the other side of the door, and he froze, knowing their laughter by heart already. Gingerly, he opened the door and stepped into the room as three pairs of eyes turned their attention to him.

"Brother!" Emma exclaimed excitedly as she stood up from the couch in the lounge area. She ran over and gave Derek a hug.

"Hey, Em." he smiled. "Um… I thought you and Reggie were going to take Taryn out today?"

"They were, but I wanted to get to know her. And when Reggie found out he had to work, I decided to fill in for him." Janie smiled as she stood up to face Derek.

"Janie." Derek sighed nervously.

"Shhh," Janie replied, holding her hand up to stop him from talking. "Before I make you spill your guts, let me just say I like this one. She's loyal, respectful, and she seems truly sincere. I like her." Janie smiled over at Taryn.

"They were amazing today, D. I had so much fun! You have the best sisters." Taryn smiled back.

"I'm glad we're all getting along." Derek chuckled. "But um… I'm kinda tired. It's been a long day. Could we…"

"Nope. They're staying. I already ordered room service to bring up dinner for all of us. You and Janie need to talk," Taryn cut in. Derek was stunned and kinda turned on by her assertiveness. "I respect you waiting to talk to her on your terms, but it put me in a bind because she was asking questions, and it wasn't my place to answer for you. Just talk to her, please?" Taryn said as her tone softened. She walked over to him, wrapping her arms around his waist.

"Okay," he replied, leaning down to kiss the top of her head. "I hope you ordered some wine too because she's going to need it," he joked, winking at his sisters. They smiled at him as they saw how truly happy he was with Taryn in his arms.

After a quick shower, Derek, Taryn, and his sisters sat down in the lounge area of the hotel room to eat dinner. Taryn had ordered them all grilled salmon with some garlic mashed potatoes and steamed asparagus. This was definitely Janie's recommendation. Derek smiled to himself as he plopped down with his plate next to Taryn on the sofa. Emma was sitting cross-legged on the floor next to the coffee table, and Janie was in the love seat off to the side.

"So what do you want to know?" Derek sighed.

"Everything." Janie scoffed. "I'm kinda hurt that our baby sister knows more than I do. How am I supposed to look after you two if you keep me in the dark about everything?" she added, her eyes going between Derek and Emma.

"We're adults now, Janie. We got this," Emma said, her mouth full of salmon.

"Yes, you inspire a real vote of confidence in my books with that face right now, Em." Janie laughed as Emma rolled her eyes before turning her attention back to Derek. "So spill it."

On a heavy sigh, Derek summed up the past few months, telling his sister everything staring with the night they met and how Lexie showed up for one last screw session right before she got married. Derek could see Janie's face twist in disgust, hearing that she had kissed Derek with Taryn witnessing everything.

"That fucking tramp!" Janie interrupted. "You're an idiot for even letting her get close to you, D. What were you thinking?"

"It's okay, we figured it out, and it was all a huge misunderstanding. We've gotten past it," Taryn answered for him, squeezing some support into his thigh.

"Yep. We figured it out after this one flew back to Hawai'i," Derek said as he looked to Taryn, her eyes dropping to her plate. "After she saw that, she had a rough phone call and had to fly home to deal with stuff."

"What stuff?" Janie pressed.

"Stuff with my ex-husband." Taryn sighed heavily.

"Wait, more than what you already told me?" Janie questioned.

"Yeah, you could say that," Taryn said, shaking her head before going through the details of her trip home. She explained why she got her divorce and continued with tear-filled eyes about how the truth of their divorce finally came out after a year.

"Why would you cover for him like that? After all he put you through, Taryn? I don't understand" Janie questioned.

"I don't either, but she just has a good heart like that." Derek smiled at her as he kissed her on the cheek.

"So after that, you guys were okay? How did you fix things? Because I wouldn't have forgiven you for kissing your ex if I were Taryn." Janie seemed to get more confused as she thought about the details.

"We weren't okay after that. Derek actually flew to Hawai'i after my student committed suicide on campus. I was a wreck," Taryn said, taking a deep breath.

"Wait, you went to Hawai'i? When? And wait, what? Your student committed suicide?" Janie was frantic, her eyes wild.

"And Taryn was the one who found his body," Derek added.

"What the Actual Fuck!" Janie exclaimed.

"Seriously, what the hell? I didn't even know this part!" Emma chimed in.

Taking a deep breath, Taryn went through the details with Janie and Emma, both of them completely encompassed by her story. Derek was now the one with his hand on her knee, giving her the comfort and support she needed as she relived one of the worst moments of her life up until that point. By the end of her story, Janie was crying, and Emma was a complete blubbering mess.

"Oh my!" Janie teared, her breath catching. "I'm so sorry, Taryn. You poor thing!"

"It's okay. Don't pity me. Pity kids like Marvin who feel they have no way out except taking their own lives. That's what's truly sad." Taryn sighed.

"Derek, I'm so proud of you for growing balls and being there for her! Good job!" Janie said, wiping her tears from her face and reaching across to slap her brother's shoulder.

"Yes, our little D is all grown up now!" Emma added, laughing through her own tears.

"Yeah, yeah. Shut up. Very funny, guys," Derek teased.

"I see why you guys got so close now. It all makes sense," Janie contemplated.

"Well…" Taryn started, looking over at Derek.

"That's not all," he finished for her.

"There's more? What more could life have thrown at you? That's crazy!" Janie was flabbergasted. "Are you talking about you running home to Mom and Dad when Lexie was murdered? I knew about that, that's why."

Taryn nodded at Derek for him to continue. Janie was not ready for the bomb he was about to drop on her.

"After Lexie was murdered and I went back to San Fran, we found out we were pregnant," Derek said cautiously as he watched his sister's face turn from confusion to excitement. Silence filled the room as Janie processed the information.

"Oh my goodness! You're pregnant? I'm going to be an aunt? Ahhh!" Janie got up excitedly. It took her a few seconds to realize no one else was celebrating. She suddenly stopped and turned concerned eyes toward Derek and Taryn.

"We had a miscarriage," Taryn's voice cracked as she swallowed hard. "A little more than two weeks ago."

Janie froze as she slowly lowered her body back into the love seat. Her mouth was ajar, and her eyes were wide, with a thousand emotions flashing across them. She opened her mouth to speak, but nothing came out.

"It's okay, Janie. We're coping with it. That's why she's here with me this weekend while I film. We needed a little getaway to get our minds off things," Derek reasoned with a forced smile, trying to suppress his own tears.

"I'm so sorry for the both of you," Janie finally spoke. "I'm such an idiot."

"It's okay." Taryn smiled through her tears. "It makes me feel really good to know you'd be so happy to an aunt to our baby."

"Whenever that is, I will be ecstatic for you both, and I will love and support that baby with every breath in my body." Janie leaned forward and took Taryn's hand in her own.

"Me too! You're already family, Ti," Emma said, getting up from the floor, squeezing herself onto the couch between Taryn and Derek. Throwing her arms over their shoulders, she exclaimed, "I love you, guys!"

After talking with his sisters and seeing Taryn's strength through it all, Derek felt lighter as if a weight had been lifted from his shoulders. It had been about an hour since they left, and room service had already come to pick up the cart, with their empty plates and dirty dishes. Taryn was in the bathroom getting ready to take a shower, and Derek just wanted to be with her.

Opening the door to the bathroom, steam hit him in the face as he blinked through it to find her. Her clothes were on the ground, and he could hear her humming to herself as the water hit the tile floor. Derek smiled to himself, already comforted by her presence. Quietly, he stripped down and stepped into the shower behind Taryn as she was rinsing her hair.

"I love you," he whispered into her ear from behind as he snaked his arms around her waist, his hands gliding across the wet skin of her tummy. Instead of startling like normal when he was being stealthy, Taryn sunk back into his embrace. The warmth of her body was pressed into Derek as he squeezed her tighter against him, the water continuing to pour down around them. Taryn turned her body in his arms as their wet skin slipped against each other.

"I love you too." She smiled as she tiptoed, pressing her lips to his gently. On instinct, Derek's arms pulled her closer as hers wrapped around his shoulders. With their noses still touching, Taryn broke their kiss and whispered onto his lips, "Thank you for an amazing weekend."

"We still have half the weekend left," he said as he smiled down at her.

"I know, but no one's ever done something like this for me, and I'm grateful beyond words." She smiled.

"I'm grateful to have had you here when I explained myself to Janie. You held your own with her today." He sighed as they both let out a little laugh. "And... I'm grateful to have you in my life, period, Taryn Okata. I don't know how I made it this far in life without you."

"Ditto." She smiled. "Even if you seemed to be doing just fine before I came along," she added teasingly.

Derek pretended to scoff as if he were offended by her comment before breaking out into laughter and crashing his lips onto her neck ravenously, biting and nibbling as Taryn squirmed, smiling in his arms.

"D!" She giggled as she writhed in his grip. "Stop, you're making me laugh so hard my tummy is hurting!"

"Nope. Not until you admit you've made my life better," he argued, with his face buried in the crook of her neck, his arms wrapped tightly around her body.

"Okay! We've made each other's lives better." She laughed as he continued his attack. "Before you, I didn't even think I'd ever smile again, but you brought happiness back into my life, and I can't imagine it without you now." Her words were choked out as her laughter turned serious.

Derek suddenly stopped and stared down at her. The water had matted her hair to her face, and he couldn't tell if the droplets of water on her cheeks were tears or if they were from the shower. Taking one hand, he brushed the water from her face as she took a deep breath.

"I never thought I could feel this way about someone, Derek. What I feel for you goes beyond anything I've experienced in the past, and it scares me half to death," she choked. "But I'm done fighting it. Whatever this is, wherever it takes us, I'm in it for the long run. And if it leads me to getting my heart broken again, so be it. The time I'm lucky enough to have with you will all be worth it."

Derek's heart jumped into his throat as sincerity poured from Taryn's eyes. He had never had someone open up to him about their feelings for him or had he ever had someone say he was "worth it." Granted Lexie was his only ex, but she always made him feel as if he wasn't worth anything, that everything he had done or tried to do for her was never good enough. So to hear Taryn just say that had his heart melting in his chest. Unable to find the words to respond, he lifted her to his body, her legs finding their spot wrapped around his waist. Sitting with her on his lap on the shower bench, he ran his hands up her back, her toned muscles tensing under his touch. On a grateful sigh, he finally spoke.

"I don't know what the future holds for us, Taryn, but know when I promised you I wasn't going anywhere, I meant it. I know we've been through a lot already, and I will spend the rest of my life making up for every ounce of hurt your heart has ever experienced. I want to fall asleep next to you every night, wake up next to you every morning, and obsess over thoughts of you throughout the day. I know you said you're scared, honestly, I am too. But I love you with a passion that runs deep into my soul, and I'll use every breath in my body to prove it to you until my heart gives out." Pulling her into his chest, Derek felt complete, as if he had finally found the missing piece of his heart he never knew he needed until now. He was finally home in her arms.

32

Nathan

It was late on Sunday afternoon. Nathan and Taryn's parents would be leaving in the morning, so he was cooking one last family dinner for them to share. Sienna was prepping the salad as Nathan went through the motions of frying the bites of chicken breast and dipping them in the family's sesame-brown-sugar-soy-sauce recipe. Tiana and Noah were sitting on the couch, hooked on the Nintendo Switch game they were introduced to over the weekend.

"We need to get one of these for the house when we head back home!" Tiana laughed as her whole body moved with the controllers.

"Why? So you can keep losing?" Noah laughed as he nudged her with his shoulder. They were like two kids stuck in adults' bodies sometimes. Nathan just laughed hearing his parents play-fight.

"Hey, guys," Taryn said as she opened the door to the apartment. "We're back." She smiled. It was the first time Nathan had seen her smile since before she had lost the baby.

"Welcome home, Ti!" Sienna smiled as she continued to chop lettuce and tomatoes. "Where's Derek?"

"He's parking the car. He should be up in a few," Taryn replied. "Hi, Mom! Hi, Dad!" she exclaimed.

"Yeah…hi. Give me five more minutes to beat your dad," Tiana said, without even glancing over her shoulder. Taryn gave Sienna and Nathan a questioning look.

"Nintendo Switch. I think they're addicted." Sienna laughed, shaking her head.

"Hey, everyone," Derek said as he entered the apartment, standing behind Taryn with a smile and kissing the top of her head.

"How was it? She died for Haunted Mansion, right?" Nathan said over his shoulder with a smile.

"I can't believe you helped him plan that and didn't tell me. You know I hate surprises," Taryn said to her brother.

"Hey, but it was a good surprise, right?" Nathan retorted.

"Yes, it was," Derek said, wrapping his arms around Taryn's waist, resting his head on her shoulder. "Thank you for all the suggestions. It was amazing."

"Glad I could be of help." Nathan smiled.

"Save all the oofing for after we all go to bed, please," Noah joked as Tiana turned off the game, and they came into the kitchen. "We want a shot at another grandkid, but we don't want to see how it was made."

"Dad!" Taryn chuckled, embarrassed.

Everyone broke out into laughter. Everything was finally getting back to normal, and whatever happened down in LA with Derek seemed to have brightened Taryn's spirits, and Nathan was grateful for it. Despite the ups and downs, this summer was one to remember. It brought Nathan closer to his family than ever, and he was excited to see what the future had to offer.

33

Derek

It was Taryn's last week in the Bay. She had just wrapped up teaching her college courses and had one week to enjoy the city before having to go back home to Hawai'i. Derek had spent every second he wasn't on set with Taryn since they got back from LA. From date nights to late nights lost in each other, they were inseparable. Luckily, they wouldn't be spending their last week together moving too much stuff.

Since Nathan and Sienna couldn't find a reasonable place to rent that wasn't ridiculously far from work and school, they came to an agreement with Derek's dad. They could stay in the apartment and rent it from him for a year at a discounted price as long as Nathan helped to manage Mr. Bennett's other rental properties in the Bay area. Nathan and Sienna would need to check on the tenants and put them in touch with appropriate resources for repairs if needed at least once a month. In return, they could remain in the three-bedroom apartment for a steal!

"Thank your dad again for us please," Nathan said to Derek as they sat drinking coffee, waiting for the girls to come out. "His generosity is a blessing and a half! We would never have found somewhere like this to rent for such a reasonable price."

"Of course! It's not a problem. You're practically family already." Derek smiled.

"What is this I hear about being a family?" Sienna questioned as she entered the kitchen area.

"Well, you were like a protective older brother to Emma through college, and now I can't see myself without Taryn. So we're pretty much linked for life," Derek teased.

"Don't get ahead of yourself." Nathan sighed. "Even if it seems like we've known each other for years, you and Taryn have barely been together officially for more than a few months. Don't rush it. I know my sister. She'll run if she gets spooked."

"I won't. But I promise you, I'm not going anywhere." Derek gave Nathan a reassuring smile. "I'm going to check on Taryn. I wonder what's taking her so long."

Getting up from the table, he headed into her bedroom to find the bathroom door closed. Usually, if her bedroom door was closed, she would leave the bathroom door open. If she really needed privacy, she would just lock the bedroom door. Something didn't seem right. Turning the doorknob slowly, Derek entered the bathroom as his eyes scanned the room for evidence of her. Just as he was about to call out for her, she emerged from the separate door leading to the toilet. Standing there quietly, he waited for her to notice him.

"Fuck!" Taryn said, grasping the doorknob behind her back with one hand and her chest with the other. "Geez. You scared me."

"Are you okay, baby? Your cheeks are a little flushed?" Derek stared at Taryn. She seemed jumpier than usual. Lately, his ninja-like ways didn't even scare her anymore. So the fact that she was jumpy all of a sudden had him concerned.

"I'm fine, just had a sore tummy. That's all." Taryn smiled. "I'll be out in a five?"

"Okay." Derek sighed, placing a hand gently on her shoulder and kissing her forehead. "I'll be in the kitchen. We have brunch reservations with Emma and Reggie, remember? I got a surprise for you, guys."

"Sounds good. I'll be right there." Taryn smiled nervously as she remained in place.

On a nod, Derek turned and left her, wondering what they ate that could have upset her stomach. Hopefully, she'll be okay to get through brunch with everyone. He had big news to share with them but was more concerned about Taryn than himself at this point. Giving her the space she seemed to need, he exited the bedroom and plopped down at the table next to Nathan.

"She'll be out soon." He smiled to everyone.

34

Taryn

Taryn held her breath with wide eyes as she stared at Derek who seemed to be watching her closely. She had just come from the toilet, and her heart was clenching in her chest.

"Are you okay, baby? Your cheeks are a little flushed?" Derek stared at Taryn with concern.

"I'm fine, just had a sore tummy. That's all." Taryn smiled. "I'll be out in a five?" She could feel her heart thud against the walls of her chest, threatening to break free, hoping Derek wouldn't question her further and leave her be.

Her silent prayers were answered as he reminded her about brunch before turning to leave. Taryn held her breath until she heard the bedroom door shut. Rushing to the door of the bathroom, she closed and locked it. Letting out a heavy sigh, she braced herself on the counter as she placed the plastic stick down on the counter. Two bright, defined red lines filled her vision as her eyes began to blur with tears. She was pregnant again.

"Wow," was all she could say to herself as she tried to compose her emotions. Just over a year ago, she was told it would basically be a miracle if she were to ever get pregnant. Then she started summer being pregnant, had a miscarriage halfway through, and now might be pregnant again? Her thoughts were reeling inside of her head as she tried to comprehend everything. Was this even possible? It had to be a mistake. Sitting on the edge of the bathtub, she pulled out her phone and googled it.

"Sex isn't recommended for at least two weeks after a miscarriage to prevent infections. However, ovulation does typically begin two weeks after loss of pregnancy, at which point a new pregnancy is possible. Miscarriages can take its toll on the mother; therefore, doctors recommend waiting until a woman is emotionally and physically ready to become pregnant again before trying."

"Okay. So it is possible. What the fuck am I supposed to do now?" Taryn said aloud to herself on a panicked breath.

She was leaving San Francisco to get back to her life in Hawai'i in a week. If her first pregnancy with Derek had stuck, they would've had all summer to figure out how they would make raising a child together work when they were an ocean apart. Was it crazy of her to consider uprooting her life to be with and raise a child with a man she's only known for a few months? She did love him, and she wanted to be with him, but she figured she'd have time to navigate the whole long-distance relationship thing with an actor that's constantly traveling. How would they make it work now? This was too much too fast for her to handle again. The walls around her were beginning to close in as she felt her blood pressure rise and her pulse race. She needed time, just a little space, to figure out what to do. Hopefully, she could hold it together long enough to get through brunch with everyone.

35

Derek

Derek was just about to go back to the room to check on Taryn when she appeared in her doorway.

"You okay, Ti?" Nathan asked, his voice concerned.

"Yeah. I'm fine. I think I had too much coffee or something yesterday. Woke up, and my stomach is just really upset," Taryn said with a smile.

"Well, if you're bombing the toilet, just make sure you spray. For a chick, your ass stinks!" Nathan laughed. Taryn just glared at him playfully.

"You sure you're okay? We don't have to do brunch if you're not up to it. Or Emma and Reggie could always just come over, and we could order in." Derek tried to reason with her, knowing that she was just trying to put on a brave face for everyone else.

"I'm fine. I promise. Besides, this 'big news' sounds like something really great, and we need to be in a proper setting to celebrate whatever it is you're going to share with us." Taryn smiled, encouraging Derek.

"Okay, but if you need to come back home, just say so and we can leave," Derek said as he rubbed her arm. Taryn nodded in agreement as he grabbed his phone and keys off the kitchen counter. "I'll bring my car around. Meet you guys in the front," Derek said as he headed out the door.

36

Nathan

"You have two minutes to spill what the fuck is really going on with you before we have to head down to meet Derek. Start talking," Nathan said sternly to Taryn, taking her by surprise.

"Whatever it is, we won't say anything. If you're getting cold feet about a long-distance relationship, it's understandable. Just clue us in at least so we can have your back on whatever it is, Ti. We got you. We're family," Sienna said gently with concern.

Nathan stared at his sister, watching her demeanor change. Taryn's eyes were darting around the room, trying to avoid eye contact as she fidgeted with her purse strap.

"Taryn?" Nathan emphasized her name, trying to pull her back to reality. "What's going on?"

Dropping her eyes to her purse, Taryn sighed heavily as she opened the zipper and pulled out something wrapped in toilet paper. As she revealed it to them, Sienna gasped next to Nathan and grabbed his forearm for stability. It was now clear what was weighing on Taryn's mind.

"You're pregnant?" Sienna whispered excitedly. "Again? Is this real?"

"I'm pregnant." Taryn sighed heavily. "Please don't tell Derek. Just not yet."

"I thought you couldn't?" Nathan asked, confused.

"With my PCOS, that's what I thought, too, but he must have some strong swimmers because this is twice with him already." Taryn was exasperated by the thought.

"Or it could mean that he's the one you're meant to be with." Sienna smiled.

"Okay, wait. Why don't you want Derek to know?" Nathan suddenly thought aloud.

"One, it's a drugstore pregnancy test. These things give false readings all the time, so I want to confirm it with my ob-gyn back home first. Second, I want to give it some time to see if this pregnancy will actually stick. I don't want to get his hopes up again only to destroy them with another miscarriage. I think he was more devastated than I was when we lost the baby earlier this summer," Taryn began to explain.

Nathan thought back to how torn Derek was. Even if he was a rock for Taryn, Derek would always call Nathan and cry to him about how he would've given anything to be a father to Taryn's baby. The devastation angle Taryn was coming from was point on.

"Okay, those are reasonable. But I know you, Ti. You have that look on your face where you're telling me but not really telling me what you're thinking," Nathan confronted his sister. He knew her too well, and he knew, even if she was sounding reasonable in not wanting Derek to know yet, there was more to not telling him than she was letting on.

"Um…" Taryn sighed uncomfortably.

"Spill it, Taryn. *Now.* Or I'll go down to Derek and tell him," Nathan threatened.

"I don't want to tell him because I don't know if I want him to know…like at all," Taryn said meekly.

"What? What the fuck do you mean!" Nathan exclaimed. "He's the father. He has to know!"

"Just hear me out, please?" Taryn pleaded, checking the time on her phone. If they didn't go down soon, Derek would come up looking for them. "We aren't even sure how to do this long-distance relationship with just the two of us. Adding a baby into the mix would just complicate things more. On top of that, his acting career is booming. After he finishes filming this Netflix series next week, he's going back to LA with countless auditions lined up already. I wouldn't want him to give up everything he's worked so hard for because I'm pregnant, and you know he would. Plus, I'm more than capable of taking care of the baby by myself back home. I just want us to figure our relationship out before either of us makes any rash decisions just because I'm pregnant. I don't want him making decisions based on that alone."

"So you're just never going to tell him?" Nathan was shocked. "Your reasoning just went from understandable to absurd, Ti. You sound crazy."

"No, I don't! When you care about someone, you just want what's best for them even if that means putting yourself in the back seat of their life," Taryn argued.

"And how do you know what's best for him, huh? How do you know he wouldn't choose you and this baby over his career?" Nathan retorted.

"He shouldn't have to choose!" Taryn cried.

"So you're choosing for him?" Nathan scoffed.

Taryn couldn't say anything. She just stood there, hanging her head. Her shoulders were heaving as she tried to control her breathing and prevent herself from crying.

"That's not fair to him, Taryn, and you know it," Nathan scoffed. "I can't believe you…"

The opening of the door cut him off as the three of them turned to find Derek with a questioning look on his face. Taryn's hand shoved the pregnancy test back into the depths of her purse as she pasted a fake smile on her face.

"Is everything okay?" Derek asked cautiously.

"I don't know. Is everything okay, Ti?" Nathan said sarcastically, earning him a slap in the arm from Sienna.

"It's her choice. Shut up," Sienna whispered in his ear.

"Yes, we're fine. Just arguing about whether or not they should move into my room once I leave for the summer," Taryn said, smiling as she walked toward Derek.

"Okay…the car's running. Let's go," Derek said as he turned on his heels and headed back down the stairs.

"Say a word, and I'll beat your face in, Nate," Taryn threatened through clenched teeth.

"Don't worry, Ti. I'll make sure he doesn't," Sienna responded before Nathan could.

With minutes, they were piled into Derek's car and heading toward downtown for brunch. Taryn was acting like herself again, smiling and making jokes. Nathan just sat in the back seat silent, unable to wrap his mind around Taryn's insistence on not telling Derek while feeling sorry for him at the same time that he might be a father again but not even know it.

37

Taryn

"It's so good to see you again!" Emma exclaimed as she embraced Taryn.

Derek had made reservations in a small, private meeting room at the Cheesecake Factory in Union Square. Emma and Reggie had already been waiting for them by the time they had gotten there.

"It's good to see you too, Em" Taryn smiled.

"Bro!" Nathan exclaimed as he shook Reggie's hand. "How's SoCal been? Hotter? You looking a lot tanner now." Nathan laughed.

"Funny, Nate." Reggie chuckled. "It's actually going really well. I'm enjoying it very much." Reggie was standing in his typical, awkward dad stance with his khakis and flannel shirt tucked in that made Taryn giggle beside herself. Aside from Sienna, Reggie was the youngest of the group yet acted as if he was seventy years old already. "Hey, Sienna. You keeping this knucklehead in line?"

"Sometimes." Sienna laughed. "Without you, he's got no boundaries. I don't know how to control this kid," she added jokingly.

"Yeah, I miss my live-in dad!" Nate joked, playfully punching Reggie in the shoulder.

"Sorry we're late, guys." Derek sighed as he headed over to the table.

"It's my fault. I wasn't feeling well this morning. I think I'm becoming lactose intolerant or something. My tummy was really

166

upset from all the coffee I had yesterday," Taryn interrupted uncomfortably as she sat down next to Derek. She didn't want him to make up some lie on her behalf.

"Don't worry, Ti. We just chillin'," Reggie said with a smile.

As they all sat down for brunch, Derek seemed to become more and more nervous. Taryn placed a hand gently on his thigh, giving it a squeeze. A waiter entered the room and began passing out mimosas. Everyone took their glass, except Taryn, as they relaxed into their seats. Sienna and Emma were chitchatting about some new influencer scandal while Reggie and Nathan caught up.

"Are *you* okay now?" Taryn whispered over to Derek as everyone else continued their own conversations.

"Yeah, I'm just excited that's all. How are you feeling?" he replied, giving her hand a squeeze. "You not drinking?"

"I'm okay. I promise. I just don't want to upset my tummy more," she said, leaning forward and kissing him on the cheek. "So what's this news you're dying tell us?"

With a smile, Derek took a deep breath, grabbed his glass, and clinked it with a fork. Standing up next to Taryn, he turned his attention to the rest of the table.

"If I could get your attention, please?" Derek said, his voice shaking. "I've got some news that I wanted to share with you guys, the most important people in my life aside from my parents," he began nervously. "After I graduated from college, I struggled trying to break into the entertainment business. By the time you're twenty-four, most actors already have made a name for themselves, so for me to start so late in the game, it was really discouraging. Getting that small part in the *Lifetime* movie in January and then one of the leads in the Netflix series that I've been shooting has been a blessing."

"Yes, and we are all proud of you. So your news is you're finally 'making it' in the industry or something?" Emma asked, confused of where this conversation was going.

"Yes, Em, I think I'm finally making it because..." Derek paused, a huge smile beamed across his face.

"Because?" Taryn asked, intrigued now.

"Because my agent got me a supporting role in a big movie that will be filmed in New Zealand for the next four months!" Derek exclaimed excitedly. "After the Netflix series wraps in August, I fly out to New Zealand to film and will be there until the first week of December!"

Taryn felt the blood from her body drain as she remained a smiling statue as everyone gave their congratulations around her. New Zealand? Filming for a movie? She knew this long-distance thing would be hard, but now to possibly add a baby into the mix… the thought alone was giving her anxiety. She definitely couldn't tell him about the baby now. If she did, he wouldn't go. He'd want to be by her side, taking care of her like a china doll until the baby came. This was too huge of an opportunity for him, and she refused to be the reason he didn't go.

"What production company is it with?" Emma asked.

"I'm not allowed to say right now," Derek was hesitant.

"D! Come on, it's us," Emma pushed.

"I know, but contractually, I'm not able to say just yet. I can tell you it's one of the biggest production companies around, and they have their own theme parks all over the world." Derek winked at his sister as he clinked his glass to hers and took a sip.

"O-M-G! It's Disney?" Emma asked excitedly.

"Or it could be Universal," Reggie reminded her as well.

"Damn! Ahhh! Well, who cares! We'll find out when we find out. I'm so happy for you, D! Congrats again!" Emma was nearly in tears with excitement for her brother.

"Thanks, Em. I'm really excited. I hope I do well because if I do, this could open up the doors to so many more job opportunities. I'm keeping my fingers crossed." Derek smiled as he turned his attention to Taryn.

She felt the hairs on her neck stand up as cold sweats took over. He could sense the nervousness on her face as he stared down at her.

"Congratulations. I'm so proud of you." She sighed, forcing a smile.

"It's New Zealand, baby. I know it's far, but I'll fly you out to come visit, and we can make sure we have time to FaceTime. Time wise, even if they're a day ahead, I'll only be two hours behind you. So when it's 8:00 a.m. your time, it'll be 6:00 a.m. my time. We'll be able to talk whenever you want to. We'll figure out how to make this work if that's what you're worried about." Derek's voice was drenched in concern.

"I'm not worried. I'm happy for you, I promise. It's just a lot to process." She sighed. Looking across the table, she could feel Nathan's and Sienna's eyes on her, waiting or urging her to say more, but she wouldn't.

"Ti, it'll be okay. My brother loves you. I know dating an 'actor' isn't traditional, but if he could stay faithful to that low-life Lexie, he'd be dumb to fuck things up with you," Emma added, trying to reassure Taryn.

Instead of comforting her, Taryn felt like now she had even more to worry about. Was she referring to him cheating? She knew as an actor and that he may have to play love interests with another woman, but being cheated on was something she only associated with her ex-husband up until this point. She didn't even put Derek into that category of man until Emma just mentioned it. This was too much to process as Taryn sat staring at her glass of water, perspiring before her on the table.

"Gee, thanks, Em," Derek scoffed, seeing more uncertainty spread across Taryn's face. Trying to change the subject, Derek tried to be encouraging, reaching for a mimosa glass and offering it to her. "Can you toast with me, baby? Please?"

Avoiding the glass of alcohol in his hand, Taryn grabbed for her own water glass and held it up to him.

"Cheers. Congratulations, Derek," she said with a warm smile, clicking her water glass to the mimosa in his hand. Seeing confusion and hurt spread across his face, Taryn added, "I'm sorry, baby. My tummy is still upset, and the smell of alcohol isn't helping right now. Congratulations though. I really am proud of you."

Derek simply nodded to himself and sat down, placing the glasses onto the table. On a heavy sigh, he opened his menu and went completely quiet. Tension grew in the room, and all conversation seemed to be halted as everyone else stared at Taryn and Derek, waiting to see what was going to happen next.

"I'm going to go to the bathroom. Excuse me," Taryn said, grabbing her purse and getting up from the table.

The second she was out the door, she could just imagine the conversation happening now that she wasn't there anymore. Derek was probably upset that she wasn't more excited for him, but she had other things on her mind. She was stuck between a rock and a hard place again. If she told him why she was distracted because she could be pregnant again, he might turn down this opportunity and resent her forever for ruining it for him. But if she doesn't, she just comes out looking like an unsupportive bitch. Add Nathan to the mix, and he might be telling Derek everything right now.

Storming into the bathroom and locking herself in one of the stalls, she sat down and tried to breathe. Tears were threatening to burst from her eyes, and she had to pull it together before everything came rushing out. Everything was getting so fucked up so fast, and Taryn could feel the anxiety taking over. Closing her eyes, she took deep breaths to try and calm herself. She had already been through so much in the past year, this was just something else she had to overcome.

"Ti? Are you in here?" Sienna's voice was gentle as it carried across the emptiness of the bathroom.

"Yes. I'm here." Taryn sighed heavily.

"Don't mind Derek. He just has this expectation in his mind of how people are supposed to react to certain things, and if it's not how he envisioned, he doesn't know how to deal," Emma's voice came over her stall door.

Taking a deep breath, Taryn stood up, wiped her cheeks, and put a smile on her face before opening the stall door. Both girls were standing and staring at her with worried looks on their faces.

"It's not, D. I'm fine. I promise." Taryn continued to smile as she headed over to the sink.

Sienna and Emma followed her over, watching carefully as Taryn placed her purse on the counter and began washing her hands. They were being extra observant as to try and see what was really going on, but Taryn refused to let her smile even budge from her face. Turning the faucet off, she moved to grab a towel and bumped into Emma, knocking over her purse, not realizing how close she had gotten in that short amount of time. The contents of her bag spilled across the floor as panic took over Taryn's entire being. She bent down and rushed to shove everything back into her purse before Emma saw. But it was too late.

"You're pregnant?" Emma asked in shock, holding the pregnancy test in her hand as she nervously knelt down next to Taryn who was now sitting helplessly on the floor. Taryn was unable to respond and simply sighed as she dropped her head.

"She found out this morning right before we left to come here," Sienna explained, kneeling down next to the two women, slowly picking up Taryn's other belongings and putting them in her purse.

Emma's eyes were locked on Taryn, and even if she wasn't looking at her, she could feel them searching her for answers.

"Derek doesn't know." Emma finally realized on a sigh.

"And you can't tell him. Please," Taryn panicked, finally bringing her eyes up to meet Emma's.

"But, Ti…" Emma began.

"No, Em! You can't say anything. After we miscarried, Derek was crushed. I don't want to get his hopes up if the pregnancy doesn't stick for sure this time. I know if I really am pregnant again, he's going to give everything up so he can monitor me in a plastic bubble," Taryn explained.

"What's wrong with that, Ti? It just shows he cares about you and his kid. That's all," Emma argued.

"Yeah. But if he does that, he'd want to be there the whole pregnancy, and…" Taryn reasoned, hoping Emma would catch the drift.

"And that means he would turn down this movie," Emma finished for her as she leaned her shoulder against the nearest stall door, letting out a heavy sigh. "Fuck."

"Exactly. This is a huge opportunity for him, Em, and I would never forgive myself if he gave that up for something I haven't even confirmed with my ob-gyn. Tests can sometimes be fake positives, you know? Plus, we haven't even figured out this long-distance relationship. I don't want to complicate things or make him feel trapped or forced to make it work just because of a baby." Taryn sighed.

"Derek doesn't deserve you." Emma laughed to herself. "You're so good to him, and he doesn't even know the half of it. Don't worry. I won't tell him, at least not until you've confirmed it, okay?"

"Thanks, Em." Taryn smiled, relieved. "For everything."

38

Derek

Why isn't she more excited for me? Did she think that actors only film in California or something? I told her we could make it work, but then she got all weird on me. Is she going to run away from me again? Derek's mind was running crazy with a billion thoughts to try and explain Taryn's bizarre behavior at brunch.

The days following brunch were awkward between Derek and Taryn. He was hurt that she didn't share the same joy he had for getting the part in the movie, and it was giving him horrible flashbacks of how Lexie would be. Was only getting the supporting role not enough for Taryn to be proud of him? Even if it was a supporting role, he was going to be the main character's best friend, so it was still a huge deal! He'd also be able to go to New Zealand for the first time in his life, and he truly wanted to share that experience with Taryn. But if she was going to act like this, their last week together, how was it going to work when they were going to be so far apart? The thoughts haunted him because he truly loved her. But was it going to work?

It was Taryn's last night in the Bay before she would be leaving to go home to Hawai'i. He arranged a beautiful evening for the two of them, but his heart wasn't in it. His thoughts were beginning to get the best of him, ruin him.

"You're all packed?" he asked as he drove them home from dinner.

"Yeah." She sighed, obviously uncomfortable with the tension that remained between them since brunch.

"Did you enjoy dinner?" he pushed, trying desperately to hold conversation with her.

"Mhm." She nodded. "Thank you for dinner."

The rest of the car ride was silent. Derek was beginning to get frustrated with her lack of effort to help him work things out. How could he figure out what she wanted from him if she refused to even hold conversation? Pulling up to the curb outside of her apartment, he put the car in park but locked the doors so she couldn't get out.

"What are you doing?" she asked, confused.

"Talk to me," Derek huffed.

"We were talking," Taryn responded awkwardly.

"No, like *talk* to me. What's going on with you? You've been in a mood since I told you about the movie," Derek snapped.

"Can we do this inside, please?" Taryn asked.

"No, because you're going to find some excuse about not wanting to fight in front of Nathan and Sienna, and we're going to end up just brushing this off," he retorted.

"Fine. What do you want to talk about?" Taryn snapped, unbuckling her seat belt and turning to face him.

"What's going on with you? Do you not want me to take the part or something? Why aren't you happy for me?" Derek argued.

"Derek, I am happy for you." Taryn sighed.

"Really? You don't show it well," Derek scoffed. "This is a huge opportunity for me. This is the biggest role I've ever been offered. I just wish I felt more support from you."

"More support? Really?" Taryn was seething, tears brimming on the edge of her eyes.

"Yes, more support. It's like you've been depressed or something since you found out that I got the part!" He was growing angry with her.

"If only you knew, Derek." Taryn scoffed. "Maybe, staying silent *is* my way of supporting you."

"If only I knew what, Ti? *Please*! Enlighten me then!" Derek exclaimed angrily.

Taryn sunk back into her seat, and silence filled the space between them. All he could hear was her breathing as she tried to control her emotions. Staring at her, he could see tears beginning to fall silently from her eyes. It broke his heart to see her so upset, but if she wouldn't talk to him, how could he make it better?

"Ti, please," he said gently as he reined his emotions in.

Still she sat there, refusing to look at him or say anything. He didn't know what to do already, and her lack of response was frustrating him even more. How were they going to make it work if she couldn't talk to him? Suddenly, his mouth was speaking, and it was too late to stop the words from coming out.

"Maybe, this isn't going to work. If you can't support me, if you can't even talk to me and be honest with me about what's going on when we're face-to-face, it won't work when we're apart." Derek sighed heavily.

Instant regret overtook him as he heard his own words hover in the space between them. Each word that came out of his mouth was an empty attempt to maintain his own composure. But before he could take it back, Taryn's voice broke its silence with one simple word, shattering his world to pieces.

"Fine," she uttered past tears that now flowed from her cheeks freely.

Manually, she unlocked her door and hopped out before he could stop her. Staring at her back in disbelief of what just happened, Derek was frozen. His world was falling apart around him as he watched Taryn walk from his view and out of his life, probably for good this time. What had he done?

39

Taryn

Taryn was still reeling over her breakup with Derek, especially after everything he said to her about how he felt and blah, blah, blah. But Taryn soon realized that words were often just empty promises, and if someone couldn't stand by you in silence, without words, they didn't deserve your praises to begin with. Especially in the case with Derek. Instead of trusting her that she supported him, the second she couldn't be what he wanted her to be, he bailed. Taryn had stood by him and learned to trust him, but when the tables were turned, yet again he couldn't trust her. He didn't trust her to be there for him when his ex was murdered, and he couldn't trust her now. Now, he was in New Zealand filming his movie, living his life with nothing and no one to hold him back.

Meanwhile, Taryn was back in Hawai'i, slowly getting her life back to normal. She had gone through tough times before, but August really tried her, some days being so bad she didn't want to get out of bed at all. Two weeks after coming home, she had gone to her ob-gyn and had confirmed her pregnancy. Nathan, Sienna, and Emma had been texting her constantly to find out whether or not she was really pregnant. Even if she had found out, she lied and told them that her doctor was booked and she wouldn't be finding out until the last week of September if she was pregnant or not. Taryn figured that giving herself that extra time was necessary in terms of deciding whether or not she was going to keep the baby. Her doctor said she would have until the last week in September to get an abortion before the baby started to develop more and aborting the pregnancy wouldn't be an option.

Taryn didn't believe in abortion, but she knew if she was pregnant and did keep it, it would somehow get back to Derek. Her life would get jumbled up in complications she couldn't even fathom all over again, in ways that she refused to bring an innocent life into. Even after what happened between them the last time she saw him, in Taryn's mind, he had no say in what was going to happen. Adoption was also an option for her, perhaps giving her baby to a couple who had been trying to get pregnant but couldn't. Maybe, even finding someone to adopt who has PCOS like her and wanted a baby. She had options, but they were all huge decisions that she needed time to make without pressures of everyone around her. And up until this point, she was lucky enough to be able to keep everything a secret even from her parents.

*****

It was the last week of September, and it was homecoming at the high school Taryn taught at. The only thing that kept her going was her students. Despite the festivities at school and her students' pleas to be there for them, Taryn took a day off to go to her ob-gyn.

"Hey, Taryn" Doctor Nelson said with a smile. He was an older Japanese man who had been the family's female doctor for three generations.

"Hey, Doc." Taryn sighed.

"So have you made a decision?" he asked as he pulled up a seat next to the patient bed.

"Honestly? No." Taryn dropped her head.

"Okay, well let's just see one more time. You know, confirm there's still a baby in there at all," Doctor Nelson joked.

"Okay." She laughed, nervously laying back on the table.

Doctor Nelson lifted her hospital gown up, exposing her tummy. The cold gel shocked her skin as he turned on the ultrasound monitor. Slowly running a wand across her tummy, her uterus came into view on the screen. Suddenly, a loud whooshing sound pulsed through the room, echoing off the walls and filling Taryn's ears.

"Yep, there's definitely a baby in there." Doctor Nelson smiled. "Heartbeat's strong too. Sounds like you got a fighter in there."

"That's the heartbeat?" Taryn choked, tears filling the corners of her eyes.

"Yes, my dear, that's the heartbeat." Doctor Nelson smiled.

"I…" Taryn dropped her head back on the table and sobbed, her hands coming up to cover her face. Doctor Nelson turned the monitor off and took a deep breath as he sat next to her.

"Taryn, can I be real with you?" Doctor Nelson sighed as he peeled her hands from her face. "You are one of my babies. I delivered you, saw you grow up, and now you're pregnant with a baby of your own. I know it's scary, but…it's a miracle. Especially after your miscarriage earlier this summer. Someone in the universe really wants you to be a mom, Taryn."

"But, Doc, I don't think I can. I'm so messed up, like what kind of mom could I possibly be?" She sobbed.

"A great one. Despite what you've been through, you are strong, resilient, and have the biggest heart. This baby is going to be so loved and is so lucky to have you as it's mommy. I have faith in you, Taryn. Just believe in yourself," Doctor Nelson reasoned. "So what's it going to be?"

Silence filled the room for what seemed like eternity as she thought about everything Doctor Nelson said.

"I guess I'm going to be a mom." Taryn sighed, smiling through her tears.

"That's my girl. Get dressed, and I'll have the print out of your ultrasound ready for you to pick up at the nurse's station." Doctor Nelson beamed with pride.

"Congratulations, Taryn," his nurse said as she handed Taryn a towel to wipe the gel off her tummy.

Sitting up on the bed, Taryn thought about her decision. Despite the fear dwelling inside of her telling her to run from this too, it was the right decision for her to make. She deserved to be happy after everything she had been through, and the idea of having this baby, a baby that she never thought she'd have, let alone have a second chance at having, made her happy. She would finally be able to pour her love into someone and have them love her back unconditionally. She finally had someone to truly live for.

40

Derek

Derek had been filming nonstop since getting to New Zealand, being on set for up to twenty-one hours on a short day. It was exhausting, but he was loving it. The long hours distracted him from the aching feeling he had in his heart every time he got a moment to breathe. He lost himself in his character, trying to escape his mistakes in real life. On set, Derek was a rock star, molding his character into whatever he needed to be. But off set, Derek turned into the recluse loner that refused to explore New Zealand with the rest of the cast and would just spend his free time alone locked up in his hotel room.

Derek was missing Taryn terribly, and he would give everything in his power to take back the words he said to her that night. He should've gone after her at least, but something in him refused to let him do it. Maybe, it was his own selfishness, or maybe, it was because he knew she was better off without him anyways. Based on her Instagram posts since she had been home, she seemed to be a lot happier. Once, around Labor Day, he picked up the phone and called her, but it went straight to voice mail. Just hearing her voice recording, made his heart skip a beat.

It was around noon when the director called cut for lunch. Derek meandered his way to his trailer and plopped down on the couch to enjoy some of the air conditioning. Taking his phone off the charger, he noticed he had a missed call from Taryn. Adrenaline suddenly pumped through his veins as he got excited just seeing her name on his screen. She had finally called him! It took her almost a month to return his call, but he didn't care. Maybe, she was missing him too? Quickly, he dialed her number, pleading with the gods for her to answer. But it went straight to voice mail, and his heart sank.

"Fuck," he said as he threw himself back on his couch.

On a heavy sigh, he looked back at his phone, and he had a new text message from Emma. As he opened it, his eyes grew wide as a black-and-white picture appeared on his screen. Was his sister pregnant? No, she would've called him to tell him, not just text the ultrasound picture. Zooming in, the name at the corner of the photo sucked the air from his lungs as he blinked back tears. In clear black letters, the name read *Taryn Okata*.

"This has to be the old one," Derek said aloud to himself as he frantically searched the ultrasound for a date: *September 25, 2019.*

The date at the bottom corner consumed Derek's thoughts as he tried to wrap his mind around what all this meant. Taryn was pregnant again. Derek's heart began to pound rapidly in his chest as he frantically dialed Taryn's number again and again, each time his call going straight to voice mail.

"Fuck, Taryn! Just answer!" he yelled at his phone before dialing Emma.

"Hello?" his sister answered casually after a few rings.

"Taryn's pregnant?" Derek's voice was shaking.

"Yes," Emma said curtly. "And it is yours by the way. She actually found out before brunch that day. *That's* why she was acting weird."

"Wait… WHAT? You knew?" Derek exclaimed.

"Yeah, I found out when I followed her to the bathroom that day at brunch." Emma seemed so nonchalant about it.

"Again WHAT?" Derek was beginning to get angry.

"It wasn't my secret to tell, and she made very plausible arguments as to why she didn't want you to know, at least not until she could confirm it with her doctor and not just a pee-pee test," Emma tried to reason.

"Really? What argument could she possibly make to not tell me that I'm going to be a dad?" Derek snapped.

"She was trying to support you, D. She knew if she told you, you wouldn't have taken that movie deal, and it was too big of an opportunity for you to turn down. Plus, with the long-distance crap, she didn't want you over-worrying or doing something crazy just because she was pregnant. She was thinking about you," Emma explained.

Everything started to make sense. Her behavior that last week, her refusal to tell him what was bothering her. She wasn't being unsupportive. Her not telling him about the baby was her way to decide for him what was best and make sure he was making the right decision to help prosper his career.

"Why are *you* telling me this?" Derek asked. "Why won't she just talk to me?"

"Well, she figured since you'd didn't go after her after you dumped her and the fact that it took you weeks to even call her, you wouldn't care," Emma scoffed. "And she said she did try to call you, just to let you know. But each time, she hung up after two rings because she couldn't bring herself to talk to you again. Something about if she heard your voice she would cave?"

"I don't understand," Derek asked confused.

"Look, D, from her perspective, she's doing what's right for the baby. You said all this stuff about you loving her and you're always going to be there only to bail on her yet again when you should've just trusted her instead of being selfish. You can't be flaky like that when you have a kid, and besides, Taryn didn't want to you to feel obligated to stay only because she was pregnant," Emma reasoned.

"Then why even tell me?" Derek asked. "Why not keep it a secret?"

"I guess her friend Lewis? Yeah, he told her that every dad has a right to know that he has a kid out there and that it should be up to the dad how involved or not involved he wants to be in his kid's life," Emma stated bluntly.

"Why won't she talk to me about it then?" Derek huffed, frustrated.

"Would you talk to you after everything you put her through? I love you, brother, but I wouldn't have even told you if I were in Taryn's shoes." Emma sighed heavily. "Look, D, you just gotta give her time. At least you know."

"I guess. Thanks, Em, for telling me." Derek sighed. "Can you do me a favor, please?"

"Depends," Emma replied hesitantly.

"Please, tell her to talk to me. Em, I still love her and haven't stopped thinking about her. I want her in my life. I just need her to know that. Would you, please, tell her for me and get her to talk to me?" Derek pleaded.

"I'll ask her to talk to you, but you have to be the one to tell her that stuff yourself. You need to apologize for being a dick, too, and for not trusting her. She was going to tell you. She just didn't want to get your hopes up if it was a false positive. But bottom line, Derek, if you do really love her, prove it to her. Right now, it only seems like you feel like that because she's pregnant. You need to feel that way about her with or without a baby in the picture, D. It's not fair to Taryn." Emma sighed.

"You're right. It does only sound like I want her in my life when she's pregnant, huh?" He laughed nervously. "But I do love her with my entire being. I'm just not good at this relationship stuff. I was only with Lexie for crying out loud, and that just taught me how to be fucked up."

"You got that right." Emma laughed. "But seriously, Derek. You're either in or you're out. You can't do that to your kid, okay?"

"I promise I'm all in, Em. I just need her to talk to me. Thank you." Derek smiled.

"Okay. I'm so excited to be an aunt!" Emma said as she hung up the phone. "I'll talk to you later. Bye!"

Derek sat back into his chair as he placed his phone on the couch next to him. Joy spread throughout him as he began to process the conversation he just had. Taryn cared about him so much that she sacrificed her own happiness so he could pursue his dreams. But now as he glanced down as the ultrasound, his dreams were slowly changing. He was going to be a dad!

41

Taryn

Months had passed since Taryn decided to keep the baby and announced to everyone that she was pregnant. She called Derek from the doctor's office after deciding but hung up after the line started ringing. Since her attempted call, she hadn't heard from Derek. Emma said she had spoken to him and pleaded with Taryn to talk to him, to give him a chance, but she couldn't bring herself to call him again. She knew she still loved him, and her heart couldn't handle talking to him just yet without crumbling. With the pregnancy hormones, she would've been doomed and fallen back into his arms like a sucker. That is *if* he even wanted her.

Shaking the thoughts from her mind, Taryn busied herself around her kitchen, cooking up all the side dishes and desserts that she would be taking to her uncle's house for Christmas Eve dinner. After deciding she was going to keep the baby, she realized she needed more space and invested in purchasing a three-bedroom, two-and-a-half bath town house, just a thirty-minute drive from her parents. It was more central with Home Depot, Costco, Safeway, and Target with five minutes of it. Plus, they had UberEATS delivery and a ton of delicious restaurants for her to order from to fulfill any craving she could possibly get.

Taryn was content with her new place, and the nursery was coming along slowly, with her working on it a little every day after school. She was in her second trimester and wanted to get it done before her belly began popping out, preventing her from having a full range of motion. Her family, her friends, her coworkers, and even her students had all been super supportive and helpful. Everyone treated her as if she were some delicate glass doll that could break at any moment, and she was well taken care of despite being on her own to raise the baby. It was an exhilarating fear that Taryn recently began to embrace.

As she pulled the pumpkin pie bites from the oven, a knock came at her door. Her parents were meeting her at her uncle's house, Jazzy was working until five, and no one else came to visit her at her new house since she moved in. Walking over to the door, she peered through the side window carefully before swinging the door open with excitement.

"Nate! Sienna! You're here!" she exclaimed almost in tears. "I thought you guys weren't coming home until next week before New Year's?"

"Yeah, but I got some extra time off, and Sienna finished her finals early, so we're here," Nathan said, smiling as he hugged his sister. "Figured we'd swing by here first and help you with whatever you need."

"Hi, Ti! Hi, baby!" Sienna said excitedly as she bent down and spoke to Taryn's tummy, rubbing it.

"You stomach don't look pregnant. You sure you're not just getting fat?" Nathan teased.

"Shut it." Taryn laughed. "Come on in."

"Wow, Ti! This place is really nice," Nathan said in awe as they entered, and he took a look around.

"Thank you. I love the open concept. I got an office nook and powder room on this floor. The two bedrooms, a full bath, and a cute master bedroom with an en suite are all upstairs. The attached two-car garage is just past the kitchen through that door, and there's guest parking marked in red out front between the assigned stalls for the one-bedroom town houses," Taryn summed.

"I love this, Ti. Can I go look around?" Sienna asked.

"Of course. Knock yourself out." Taryn smiled. "The extra room upstairs is setup as a guest bedroom for now if you guys ever want to stay here instead of at Mom's guesthouse," she added with a wink.

"Why a three-bedroom, Ti? It's just you and the baby," Nathan asked.

"I figured if I was investing in a town house, I should invest in one that I could grow into, and eventually, if I find someone in the future and we move, this is an ideal size for a rental property. So many of the new teachers at school look for places to rent like this, so I'd always have cliental," Taryn reasoned.

"Smart. I'm very proud of you." Nathan smiled. On a heavy sigh, he continued, "Have you talked to Derek? His movie wrapped a week ago. He's back in LA now."

"Good for him, but, no, I haven't spoken to him," Taryn replied.

"He knows you know…about the baby" Nathan said.

"I know." Taryn sighed softly.

"And?" Nathan paused, waiting for her to say more.

"And… I don't need a man to take care of me or my child," Taryn emphasized.

"I know that, Ti. You've always been super independent. But he wants to be a part of your life, and he should be able to be a part of the baby's life too," Nathan reasoned.

"If he wanted to be part of my life, he wouldn't have broken up with me just for feeling unsupported. And if he wanted to be part of the baby's life, he would've put more of an effort to reach out to me after he found out about the baby," Taryn retorted.

"Taryn, how was he supposed to reach out to you when you block him from social media and block his number from your phone?" Nathan started. "You know he's been calling and texting us nonstop to get daily updates on you and the baby because you won't talk to him. He still loves you, Ti."

Taryn could feel her heart clench in her chest at those words. *He still loves you.* Tears began to burn the back of her eyes, and the air seemed to be sucked out from the room. She had to compose herself quickly and stay strong for her baby. He could say he still loved her all he wanted, but deep inside, she knew it wasn't true. If it were, he would have trusted her that day instead of running. If it were, he would have stopped at nothing to reach out to her after finding out instead of giving up like he did and relying on the younger siblings to try and fix his mistakes for him.

"By the looks of you right now, Ti, I'd say you still love him too." Nathan sighed with concern in his eyes.

"How I feel doesn't matter," Taryn retorted.

"Please, just give him one last chance, Ti, please. For my niece or nephew?" Nathan pleaded.

"For your niece." Taryn smiled as a single tear rolled down her cheek.

"It's a girl? You're having a *girl*!" Nathan exclaimed excitedly. "What the fuck!"

"What's happening?" Sienna ran down the stairs.

"Taryn's having a girl!" Nathan exclaimed excitedly.

"Ahhh! Congratulations! I'm so excited for you!" Sienna beamed as she embraced Taryn in a hug.

"That's why I made strawberry shortcake cupcakes. That's why the mashed potatoes has pink food coloring in them. Get it?" Taryn laughed, motioning to the food on her kitchen island. "I was going to announce it to everyone tonight at dinner."

"I'm so happy for you, Ti," Nathan said, joining in on the hug. "But, please, give Derek just one more chance." Nathan's tone was suddenly serious as he stared down at Taryn.

"Don't tell me what to do. I'm the older sibling, remember?" Taryn scoffed, trying to avoid the request.

"Yeah, yeah, yeah," Nathan huffed with a smile as they hugged it out in in the kitchen.

42

Nathan

After helping Taryn finish up with the sides and desserts, Nathan and Sienna placed their bags in the guest room upstairs.

"She's going to kill you when she finds out what you did, you know," Sienna reasoned.

"Yeah, well I'm hoping because I'm her 'baby' brother, she'll be quick to forgive me for it," Nathan retorted.

"She barely even wanted to talk about Derek and avoided the subject completely when you asked her to give him another chance" Sienna added.

"I know, but I need to fix this. They both love each other. Taryn's never been happier than when she was with Derek. Now that she's having *his* baby, she needs to get over her 'Miss Independent' ego and just be a family with him. I refuse to let my niece grow up being torn back and forth between the two of them," Nathan argued.

"True, but Derek has put her through a lot, Nate. What if it's better if they're apart? At least Derek knows. Isn't that good enough?" Sienna sighed.

"Put yourself in Derek's shoes though. If the woman you loved was having your baby and cut you off completely, would you be able to deal with it? And from the baby's perspective, would you be okay growing up not knowing your dad or having your mom keep you from your dad? They need to at least try, and if it doesn't work, then so be it. But they need each other right now," Nathan explained.

"Okay. I just hope this plan of yours doesn't blow up in your face, Nate," Sienna argued. "Or it won't be a 'Merry' Christmas after all."

"It won't." Nathan sighed. "At least I think it won't."

43

Derek

Being away from his family for almost five months was brutal, but not hearing from Taryn the entire time was worse. Add to that knowing he was going to be a dad but not being able to talk to Taryn about it nearly killed him. He was ecstatic when the movie wrapped and he was able to get home to LA. The second he got back, they did an early Christmas-reunion dinner with him and planned out how he was going to win Taryn back. After an extensive FaceTime call with each important person to Taryn, Derek had everyone on board to help him execute his plan to win her back. He was determined to make up for everything and then some. This time, he wasn't fighting just for Taryn, he was fighting to keep his little family together.

With constant updates from Nathan, he found out Taryn had purchased a town house for herself. She had just made her down payment in time for her to move into the house in December, and it was perfect timing for his little surprise. Derek had his dad reach out to the real estate agent who sold it to her through his connections. After multiple phone calls and emails, as a pregnancy gift without telling Taryn, Derek's parents split the remaining cost for the house with Derek. They also transferred the mortgage payments to be pulled from Derek's account instead of Taryn's.

Since Derek had been moving all around since filming at the start of the year, a majority of his things were already packed and stored in a unit in downtown LA. Depending on how phase two of his plan went, he would come back to LA to uproot himself altogether and start a new life with Taryn in Hawai'i. The town house would be theirs where they would raise their baby together. Since she could still travel until her third trimester, he would take her with him to promote his movie, and they could make it back to Hawai'i just in time for her to give birth, if she was okay with it. As far as his acting career went, he would continue to take jobs as long as Taryn agreed, and he would only leave to film for condensed periods of time, similar to short-term deployments. He prayed his reasoning and plans would work. He desperately needed her in his life. The emptiness he's felt these past few months without her was simply unbearable.

Sitting on the plane, Derek was nervous. A thousand thoughts ran through his mind as he stared out the window, dark blue ocean was all he could see out his window for miles. Derek had worked it out with Nathan to come down to Hawai'i for Christmas and the New Year. Noah and Tiana were in on the surprise, too, and were the ones who would be picking Derek up from the airport when he landed on Christmas Eve. His nerves were getting the best of him as the time seemed to fly by and the plane was suddenly pulling into the gate as they landed in Hawai'i.

"Aloha. Thank you for flying with Hawaiian Airlines. We hope you enjoy your stay, and we look forward to servicing you on future flights. Mahalo," the flight attendant's voice rang over the speakers as Derek got up from his chair and gathered his belongings.

Stepping off the plane, the sun beamed into his eyes, and the heat caused beads of sweat to form on his brow. Taking a deep breath, he walked toward the baggage claim. After about fifteen minutes, his suitcase slid down the chute, and he was heading out toward the sidewalk. He dialed Tiana's number.

"Hey, it's Derek. I'm on the curb under the BAGGAGE CLAIM 23 sign," he said when she answered.

"We see you!" Tiana replied, hanging up.

Within a few seconds, a white Toyota 4Runner pulled to the curb. Noah was driving, and Tiana was sitting in the passenger seat.

As they parked, both of them hopped out wearing matching aloha-print clothing.

"Hey, Derek. It's good to see you again." Tiana smiled.

"Hey, Mrs. Okata. It's good to see you too," Derek replied with a smile.

Without saying anything, Noah took Derek's bags and walked around to the trunk as he opened it. Placing them in and shutting it, Noah didn't so much as glance at Derek. This was expected as he had once again broken Taryn's heart. But the fact that he was still willing to help Derek win her back eased his nerves.

"Don't mind him, D. Taryn is just our baby girl, and he just doesn't want to see her hurt again if this all goes south. Ti is not one for surprises," Tiana reasoned, seeing the anxiety spread across Derek's face. "Hop in and just watch out for the trays of food. We're late already."

On a nod, Derek slid into the back seat of the 4Runner behind Tiana. The rest of the chair and the floor was covered in large silver tin pans filled with food. The mouthwatering smells of turkey, gravy, stuffing, and casseroles filled his nostrils. Taking a deep breath in, he could even smell garlic, butter, and bacon. His stomach started growling, reminding him that he had been so nervous about this trip that he hadn't eaten since lunchtime the day before. After driving in awkward silence for what seemed like eternity, Derek gathered his courage and spoke.

"Mr. and Mrs. Okata?" he started.

"Yes, Derek? You okay?" Tiana replied.

"I know I said this before, but I'm sorry. For everything. I know I don't deserve another chance with your daughter, but I want you to know that I do love her…with everything I have. I just need you guys to know that." Derek sighed.

"We know, Derek. You both are still young and just starting to advance in your careers. It's hard to think about other people when you are figuring yourself out," Tiana reasoned.

"Still that's no excuse for what I put her through," Derek replied. "I should've been there for her, pushed her more to talk to me, and tell me what was going on before. I was stupid."

"Yes, you were," Noah finally broke his silence. "But Taryn is the stubbornest person you'll ever meet. She would never budge anyways." He sighed heavily.

"You don't need to rehash this stuff, Derek. We talked it through before, and it's water under the bridge already, okay?" Tiana added.

"But," Noah spoke before Derek could respond, "don't hurt her again. This time you won't just be hurting her, you'll be hurting my grandbaby, and I won't stand for it. You understand?"

"Completely. Thank you." Derek sighed.

"Hey, third time's a charm, right?" Noah chuckled, making Tiana and Derek smile despite the obvious tension still in the air.

"Yes, honey, third time's the charm," Tiana said, resting a loving hand on her husband's knee as he drove.

As Derek watched them, he sighed with hope. With role models like his parents and Taryn's, he knew that no matter what happened after today, they were going to be okay.

44

Taryn

Taryn dropped Nathan and Sienna off at the front of her uncle's house, their cousins all meeting them at the car to help take out the food that she brought.

"I'm going to circle the block for parking. Save this one in the front for Mom and Dad," Taryn called to Nathan out her window.

"Got it!" Nathan replied before turning into the house with the pumpkin pie bites.

As she drove around the block, she found parking on the next street over. After hoping out, she checked her front bumper to make sure she wasn't blocking the driveway to the house and checked her back bumper to make sure the car behind her had enough space to leave.

"Perfect," she said to herself as she grabbed her purse and coat from her back seat and locked her car.

Despite it being Hawai'i, the temperature in her uncle's area was way colder than where she grew up. The neighborhood he lived in was up in the mountains in the center of the island as opposed to where she lived, which was at a much lower elevation and minutes from the beach. Taryn took her time to walk down the long street and over to the next where her uncle's house was. She smiled as the leaves crunched beneath her flats and inhaled the smell of dew on the air as a large gray cloud moved toward her from the distance. Rain signified a Hawai'i Christmas. It was the closest thing they got to snowfall. As she rounded the corner of the street to head down to her uncle's, she smiled as she saw her cousins' kids playing in the street with a football. Even the girls in their pretty dresses were sweating and running with the boys.

"You'll be running and playing with them when you're old enough," Taryn said to her tummy as she rubbed it lovingly, smiling at the thought of her little girl running around with all her cousins' kids.

When she was growing up, the older boys in the family often roughhoused the girls, just as a way to make sure they were tough as nails so that no one messed with them when they went to school. Skidding their knees on the gravel or getting a bloody lip from crashing their bikes was something every one of them experienced, and Taryn wouldn't have had it any other way. It instilled a physical and mental toughness in her that allowed her to survive everything over the last year.

As Taryn got closer to the house, she noticed her parents' 4Runner in front of the house now, but only her cousin's husband, Conner, was outside watching all the kids by himself. That was strange because this cousin-in-law only ever came out of the backroom during family parties to eat. He would never be caught dead watching his kids let alone watching all the kids by himself.

"Hey, Conner," Taryn said nervously. "Merry Christmas."

"Hey, Ti," he replied solemnly without looking up at her. "Everyone's inside."

"Are they eating already? Why aren't the kids inside?" Taryn asked.

"I don't know," Conner said, shrugging her off as he took a swig of his beer.

Usually at her family parties, everyone was scattered all over the place. The uncles stayed outside drinking by the grill while they watched the kids play in the driveway. The aunties were often spread, some on the sidewalk as a barrier to prevent the smaller kids from chasing their siblings into the street and others stuck in the kitchen prepping the next courses. All the cousins would be squished in the garage turned den drinking and playing pool with one another. So with no one to be found and everyone *inside*, Taryn was worried. The last time they all gathered like this was when someone had passed.

Nerves and worry, suddenly took over. Rushing down the side of the house to the entrance door, she kicked off her flats and pushed it open hurriedly. Taryn froze in her tracks as the air was sucked from her lungs and tears instantly burned her eyes. Red and green balloons hung from the ceiling for as far as she could see in the house, spreading from the entryway, to the living room and dining room, to the kitchen. Her family members were all inside, like Conner said, but each of them held a sign with either a heart on it or a letter, letters that ended up spelling out *"Will You Marry Me"* on them. Nathan and Sienna were standing off to the left with huge smiles on their faces while Noah and Tiana were to the right, tears filling their eyes. At the center of it all was Derek, he was on his knee, eyes glazed with his own tears and a huge smile on his face. Taryn's heart felt as if it were going to explode from her chest.

"What is all of this?" Taryn finally asked, her voice catching in her throat.

"Taryn, I have always loved you, and I have never stopped thinking about you. I know I've made catastrophic mistakes, but the time I spent apart from you made me realize that I need you in my life. You're the girl I want to be with forever, and if you'll let me, I will spend the rest of my life making sure every day you feel appreciated, supported, and loved. Please, do me the great honor and say you'll be my wife," Derek choked out, letting tears fall freely down his face.

Taryn had no idea what to say or how to respond. It was like something out of a fairy tale, but life wasn't a fairy tale. Derek couldn't go away for four months and know about her pregnancy without saying a word. Then suddenly coming here with all this, just expecting her to fall back into his arms? No, not this time. Without giving a response, she turned on her heels and ran. Everything was so unexpected and happening too fast for her mind to process. She couldn't deal with this right now. Tears blurred her vision as she moved across the cold pavement, numbing her bare feet. Her mind was racing faster than she could move, and the world around her started to spiral out of control as she heard footsteps coming after her, Derek calling her name in the distance. She moved to cross the road, trying to find a shortcut to her car.

The sound of a horn blazing echoed in her ears as her body seemed to move in slow motion until she was on her back, laying on the cool cement of the sidewalk, with a loud thud knocking the wind out of her. Blinking rapidly, she tried to calm her thoughts and rationalize what had just happened. *The baby.* Looking down at her body and feeling herself from head to toe, she realized she wasn't hurt. She wasn't even in the road at all. But how did she get here? Looking around for answers, her heart sank as she saw a large black Ford parked in the middle of the road, the driver side door of the truck flung open. Gingerly, Taryn peeled herself from the ground as she walked over to the truck, slowly circling around to the front. Her heart stopped altogether in that moment as she saw Derek laying there, bruised and bloodied on the ground, lifeless. Dropping to her knees, she lifted his head and placed it on her lap as tears began to fall from her eyes.

"Derek!" she cried. "No…please! No!"

"What were you thinking, lady!" the truck driver yelled at her. "What the fuck is wrong with you?"

"What happened?" Taryn panted, looking up at him.

"You ran in front of my truck, and when I honked, you froze! This dude jumped in front of me and shoved your dumb ass out of the way! What the fuck were you doing?" The driver was frantic.

"Call 911!" Taryn shouted. "Please!"

"I did. They're on their way. Just don't move him, lady!" the driver urged. "Are you okay?" he asked as his eyes drifted to Taryn's tummy.

"Just call 911. Please," Taryn pleaded with the driver.

Holding Derek's head still, she tried to wipe the blood from his face. Moving her hand to his neck, she could still feel his pulse but he was unresponsive.

"I'm so sorry. Please, don't leave me like this. I love you, Derek. I love you. Please don't leave me like this. I need you. Your baby needs you. Derek, please. Stay with us!" Taryn cried as rain began to fall around them.

"I'll take that as a yes then?" Derek said softly, taking a deep breath reaching his hand up gingerly to rest it on the hand she had placed on his chest.

"You're alive?" Taryn sobbed.

"Only if you say yes." Derek chuckled.

"Yes, Derek, yes. I'll marry you! You crazy idiot." Taryn cried in relief as she collapsed forward, leaning her forehead onto his. Closing her eyes, she took a deep breath and kissed his cheek gently, her tears kissing his skin, appreciating her touch in any way.

"I love you too." Derek sighed with a smile as he relaxed in Taryn's hold as the emergency sirens were approaching. Despite just getting hit by a car, Derek seemed happy as he lay there in the middle of the street in the pouring rain with her.

45

Derek

"Hey. She said she would marry me, you know," Derek told the EMT through the oxygen mask on his face.

"Congratulations, sir." The EMT smiled.

Derek began to fidget on the stretcher in the back of the ambulance, trying to reach for something in his pocket.

"Sir, please keep still. You could make your injuries worse if you keep moving," the EMT requested calmly.

"Derek, stop moving, or I'll come back there and make your injuries worse myself," Taryn said from the front seat.

"But I need to get it," Derek argued.

"Sir, let me help you then. What are you trying to grab?" the EMT asked, placing a hand on Derek's arm to get him to stop moving.

"In my pocket. She said yes." Derek sighed, feeling the ring box just out of his reach.

Pushing his hip out to the EMT, Derek nodded down at him to grab it. On a heavy sigh, the EMT reached into the depths of Derek's pocket and pulled out a tiny black box with gold detailing on it. Opening it up, the two-karat princess-cut diamond sparkled in the ambulance lights. Set in white gold and adorned with smaller diamonds around it and around the band, it was breathtaking, but not nearly as breathtaking as Taryn.

"Put it on her finger for me, please," Derek asked the EMT, who looked at him with awkward eyes.

"Derek, not now. That can wait," Taryn argued from the front seat.

"No, it can't. You said yes, and I don't want you to change your mind. Just let him put the ring on you woman!" Derek scoffed from the stretcher.

"We need to make sure you're okay first" Taryn retorted. "Why did you run after me? Why did you throw yourself in front of that car?"

"I'm always going to protect you and our baby." Derek scoffed. "But I would feel better if you just accept the ring. Now give this guy your hand," Derek argued back.

"You're impossible, you know that?" Taryn huffed as she turned in her seat and held out her hand to the EMT.

"And you said yes, you know that?" Derek said sarcastically as he gazed above him and watched the EMT put the ring on Taryn's finger. "Perfect fit."

"Thank you," Taryn said to the EMT.

"Do you like it?" Derek asked.

"I love it. Thank you." Taryn smiled. He could hear her words get caught up with emotion as he watched her stare at the ring.

"I love you, baby." Derek smiled.

"I love you too, you crazy idiot," Taryn replied.

"Hey, I love you guys too. You're invited to the wedding. You practically helped with the engagement!" Derek laughed as the EMTs chuckled along with him. "We're going to be okay, Taryn. It'll all be okay."

46

Taryn

"So? Is he okay?" Nathan asked over FaceTime as Taryn sat next to Derek in the emergency room.

"Yes, he's fine. Lucky we were still in a residential area and not on the main road. The slow speed of the car is what saved him. He just has a minor concussion and some bruised ribs but nothing major. X-rays all came back good. He just needs to rest. We can go home in a few hours," Taryn explained.

"And?" Nathan pushed.

"And what?" Taryn questioned.

"The proposal. We were all waiting for your response, and you just booked it without a word. Do you know how long we've been working and planning this out? Jazzy was even on board, coordinating things," Nathan huffed.

"How long have you guys been working on this behind my back?" Taryn scoffed.

"That's not important. Now come on, Ti, what did you tell him?" Nathan urged.

"I can't believe you guys kept this from me this whole time," Taryn said jokingly, lifting her hand, letting the ring sparkle into the camera in the dim lights of the room.

"You said yes!" Nathan exclaimed.

"I said yes." Taryn smiled.

"She said yes, guys!" Nathan announced to the rest of the family who was still at their uncle's house eating dinner. "Congratulations, Ti! I'm so happy for you."

"Thanks, Nate." Taryn sighed as she heard an echo of congratulations ring out in the background of the phone call.

"And congratulations on having a girl!" Jazzy's face filled Taryn's screen. "Who run the world? Us bitches do! *So* excited to meet my niece!"

"Thanks, Jazzy." Taryn smiled. "I'll call you guys when we're going to get discharged. Nate, you got my keys, right? I gave them to you before we left in the ambulance."

"Yes, I do, we'll come get you guys," Nathan said.

"And they'll have plates of food for you guys, since your dumb ass ran away and got your fiancé banged by a car before you could eat!" Jazzy yelled in the background.

"Thank you. Love you, guys." Taryn sighed.

"Love you too. See you in a bit," Nathan said as he hung up the phone.

Sitting back in the chair next to Derek, Taryn sighed and looked down at her ring. She had her own place. She was getting married. She was having a beautiful baby girl. It was all so crazy, and it filled her with joy she never knew she could feel. One year of heartache was followed by one full of happiness. Taryn could barely comprehend it all.

"We're having a girl?" Derek's voice was soft despite the silence of the room as he turned his head to her. "Our baby is going to be a 'daddy's little girl,' Taryn?"

"We are having a girl." Taryn smiled.

Tears of joy filled Derek's eyes as he reached a hand out to Taryn. Scooting closer to his bed, Taryn took his hand gently and kissed him on his knuckles.

"Thank you." Derek sighed happily, sitting up and kissing her tenderly.

"For what?" Taryn asked gently as she pulled back to look him in his eyes.

"For being the best thing to have ever happened to me," he replied simply.

In the short time that she had known Derek, they had been through so much together, seeing one another at their absolute lowest points in life while helping to build each other up and supporting one another to heights neither thought was possible. From a crazy whirlwind start, Taryn had fallen harder for him overnight than she ever had for anyone in her past. When her world crashed and shattered around her, he was there to help her pick up the pieces, taking it a day at a time, to show her how to move on with her life. And now despite the four months they had lost, she felt whole again with him by her side. He had finally healed her heart, a heart she never thought would be whole again until he stumbled into her life. She had finally found her forever.

Four months later

Since getting engaged, Derek had been her rock. He left after New Year's for a week to settle everything in LA, and within a few days of being back, he had fully moved into Taryn's town house and refused to leave her side. Seeing as he would now be based in Hawai'i for acting gigs, his agent went above and beyond, landing him a supporting role in a new Hawai'i-based cop show. Whenever he wasn't on set, he was home taking care of the house and Taryn, prepping for their little girl's arrival. On her birthday, he presented her with the title to the house, paid in full, as a gift that brought her to tears. Everything was finally going well for them, and they had developed a relationship that worked.

As Taryn got further into her pregnancy, her doctor had them come in once a week to check on the baby due to her past miscarriage. Despite this, Taryn refused to take maternity leave from work, as she neared her May second due date. It was a little over a week before, and she had just gotten home from work. Sitting at the dining room table, she put her feet on the adjacent chair to rest before starting dinner. Looking toward the door, she smiled to herself as a car seat and her overnight bag came into view.

"Any day now," she said as she rubbed her belly.

"Baby, enough already. You need to stay home and rest. This is taking a toll on your body," Derek said as he entered from the garage. Taryn hadn't even heard him come in and was zoning out in exhaustion.

"I know. We're one week away already, so my maternity leave starts now." Taryn smiled. Derek looked at her in disbelief as he put his key ring on the hook by the door. "I'm serious. Today was my last day. Sub plans are made, I coordinated with my coworker to input final grades, and I said my farewells to my kids already."

"And *you* chose to do this?" Derek asked suspiciously.

"Yeah." Taryn smirked. "No…the staff surprised me with a baby shower at our end-of-the-week meeting. I haven't gotten a chance to take the gifts out of my car yet. But my friends made my lesson plans and copies and got me a sub until the end of the year. And my vice principal did my paperwork. I just had to sign it today. So yeah, I was forced into relaxing, Derek" she added with a chuckle.

"That's more like it. Are you okay with finally relaxing?" Derek asked.

"Surprisingly, yes. I'm exhausted, and I guess knowing that I'm on leave now, my body finally gave into it, and I'm feeling this pregnancy full force now." She giggled.

"Well, as long as you actually relax, okay? I'll take care of dinner. Let's get you upstairs and have a nice soak in the tub," Derek said, helping her up from the chair and kissing her on the cheek.

"Okay. Thank you." Taryn smiled up at him. "I think until the baby comes, I'm just going to binge-watch…" A blinding pain suddenly collided with Taryn in the tummy as she folded over, squeezing Derek's hand for support, clenching onto her side with the other. "Oh," she sighed.

"Ti? Baby? What's going on?" Derek's face was full of concern.

"I'm not sure. I think it's just Braxton Hicks," Taryn said, taking deep breaths. "I've been feeling them since this morning when I got to work. I had to stop teaching here and there to take a breather. I think they're only getting worse now because I can finally relax. So I'm actually feeling them, you know?"

"Baby, you've had them all day?" Derek exclaimed. He was panicking.

"Yeah, but I think real contractions are way worse, right? This just feels like really bad cramps. The hot water should help," Taryn said, smiling as she tiptoed and kissed Derek on the nose. "Forget dinner. Come keep me company instead. We can just order takeout."

"Are you sure you're okay?" Derek asked, following her toward the stairs, holding her with one hand while supporting her lower back with the other.

"Derek, I'm fi…oh!" Taryn's voice caught in her throat as she braced herself on the counter by the stairs.

The sound of water splashing on the ground, as if a water balloon had just popped, suddenly echoed around them. As they both looked down, a large puddle spread on the floor under Taryn's feet as water continued to drip down her legs. Panic suddenly filled Taryn's eyes.

"Does this mean…" Derek spoke first in pants.

"Yeah. I think so. I've never had my water break before, but if it feels like I'm peeing and can't control it, then I think my water just broke. And if my water did break, that means the baby is coming, and she's coming like *now*," Taryn tried to reason aloud with herself as calmly as possible.

"The baby's coming?" Derek was suddenly alive.

Springing into action, he ran to the powder room, yanking a towel from the rack, throwing it on the ground between Taryn's feet. Turning again, he ran, grabbing the keys, car seat, and their night bag and loaded the car just as another contraction crippled Taryn.

"Derek!" she cried out as she folded over again, holding her tummy, barely able to stand anymore.

"I'm here, baby. Everything's in the car. I got a towel on the seat in case you're still leaking, and I've triple-checked the bag everyday so we don't forget anything," Derek urged as he ran back to her side and helped her up. His phone was already in his hand as he began timing how long the contraction was lasting. "Just breathe, baby, deep breaths. When this one passes, we'll get you in the car, okay?"

"Okay." Taryn nodded as she took deep breaths through the pain. Staring up at Derek with tear-filled eyes, she said, "We're finally going to meet our daughter."

"We're going to meet our little girl." Derek smiled back as he tenderly kissed her. "Let's get you to the car."

Standing her up, Derek walked Taryn over to the car and helped buckle her in. He took the giant U-shaped pillow they had gotten for the baby and wrapped it around Taryn's belly. She looked at him with questioning eyes as he got into the driver's seat.

"What? It's extra protection for the baby while I drive." Derek sighed nonchalantly, making Taryn smile.

"Are you ready to meet our baby?" she said as he pulled out of the driveway.

"I'm more than ready, Ti. Bring on the baby!" Derek exclaimed as they began the journey toward the hospital.

*****

After seventeen hours of labor, their little girl finally made her long-awaited arrival into the world. Their families had camped out in the waiting room, refusing to leave until they each got to see her. Nathan and Sienna had flown down two days prior with Emma, Reggie, and the rest of the Bennett family so they could be there in a moment's notice if Taryn went into labor.

Taryn's and Derek's parents were the only ones allowed in the delivery room. All four were blubbering messes from the moment their baby girl took her first breath and cried with strong, powerful lungs.

"She's...so...beautiful." Tiana sobbed, hovering over the nurse that was wiping her clean.

"That's...our...grand...baby... Tiana." Mrs. Bennett cried.

Still clenching Taryn's hand in his, Derek smiled down at her. He was filled with so much joy he had no idea what to even do anymore. Brushing the matted hair from Taryn's sweaty face, he leaned down and kissed her gently with pride.

"I love you," he whispered.

"I love you too." She sighed. She was still breathing heavy from labor.

The nurse walked back over to them with their baby girl wrapped up snuggly in a blanket and gently placed her in Taryn's arms. The warmth of the baby against Taryn's chest suddenly calmed her, and she beamed as she stared down at the little piece of life she was holding in her arms.

"I'll give you, folks, some time." The nurse smiled. "Congratulations."

"We are so lucky." She smiled. Taryn's heart felt as if it were going to explode as tears of joy filled her eyes.

"Yes, we are" Derek echoed as he rested his hand on Taryn's hand as she held the baby close.

"We're going to let everyone know she's here," Derek's dad said, clearing his throat from his own sobbing.

"Yeah, you two take a minute alone with your little girl," Noah added, wiping his own eyes.

"But we want to…" both moms tried to argue as their husbands edged them out of the room, making Taryn and Derek laugh despite themselves.

"My two girls." Derek sighed, wiping his eyes and wrapping his arms around Taryn and his daughter. "I didn't know you could love two people so much and not have your heart combust."

"I know exactly how you feel." Taryn sobbed. "I love you both so much."

They stood in the moment together for what seemed like eternity, both in complete awe of the beautiful baby girl they had brought into this world together.

Two years later

"Mommy!" a tiny voice called out from beneath the fluffy skirt of Taryn's wedding dress.

"Caylin. What are you doing my little girl?" Taryn smiled as she reached down and lifted her daughter to her hip.

"Mommy, pretty," Caylin said as she touched and poked at Taryn's hair.

"Thank you, baby. You ready to get in your pretty dress?" she asked her daughter.

"No! No dress." Caylin wiggled out of Taryn's arms and ran to hide behind Jazzy.

"If you don't put on your dress, you can't go with your mommy to see your daddy," Jazzy said over her shoulder.

"Yes, and you don't want daddy waiting *forever* for you guys, do you?" Sienna added, kneeling down next to Jazzy, trying to coax Caylin out from her hiding spot.

"Daddy! I want Daddy!" Caylin exclaimed excitedly as she ran into Sienna's arms.

"Okay, we'll let's get this dress on you then, little missy," Emma said, walking over with Caylin's tiny flower girl dress.

"Auntieeeee!" Caylin shouted, running over and jumping into Emma's arms. "Daddy! Daddy! Daddy!"

"Dress first," Emma said sternly.

"Okay," Caylin replied on a huff, sliding down the length of Emma's body. Reluctantly, she stood there, allowing Emma to change her into her flower girl dress.

"You ready for this?" Jazzy asked Taryn as she fixed a bobby pin at the back of her hair.

"More than ready." Taryn sighed. "Get me out there so I can marry my best friend."

"Bitch, I thought we were your best friends?" Jazzy scoffed jokingly.

"No, you're all my sisters, and I love you guys," Taryn retorted.

"Yeah, yeah, yeah." Sienna laughed as she gathered their bouquets. "It's time. Let's go."

As she stood with Noah and Tiana behind the doors to the ballroom, Taryn could feel her heart thudding in her chest. She was beginning to get nervous as she saw each of her bridesmaids and groomsmen walk out down the aisle. The last one out was Caylin. She held on to Mr. and Mrs. Bennett as they walked her down the aisle, helping her to scatter rose petals as she walked. Not even five seconds being out of Taryn's sight, she heard Caylin.

"Daddy!" she yelled. Suddenly, you could hear all this commotion and laughter bursting from the crowd.

"Five bucks says she saw Derek, dropped the flowers, and ran to him," Noah whispered down to Taryn.

"You win already because I know she did." Taryn chuckled to herself.

"It's your turn, baby. You ready?" Tiana asked.

"Yes." Taryn nodded. "Just don't let me fall, okay?"

"Never, sweetheart," Noah said, kissing her forehead.

As the aisle came into view, all their guests on either side stood up, and all attention was on Taryn, but she didn't care. Taryn's white satin dress seemed to be an extension of the aisle, adorned in Swarovski crystals with a long train that flowed behind her. As she began walking, Taryn's eyes instantly locked onto Derek, standing at the end of the aisle with Caylin in his arms. The magnetic force that pulled them together was still as strong as it was the first day they met, and she seemed to be drifting toward him, without any control over her body. She smiled to herself as she saw his eyes fill with joy and tears as he watched her.

"Mommy! Daddy! It's Mommy! Mommy pretty, Daddy!" Caylin squealed as she began her happy dance in his arms. Derek didn't even budge as he held their daughter firmly, with a genuine smile plastered onto his face.

"Hey, beautiful." Derek smiled as Taryn finally arrived in front of him.

"Hey, handsome," Taryn replied as Noah took Caylin from Derek's arms and went to sit down in the front row.

The pastor came out and began the ceremony. Everything went so fast and happened in a blur as Taryn and Derek were completely lost in each other's eyes.

"I love you," Derek mouthed.

"I love you," Taryn mouthed back.

"I now pronounce you man and wife. You may kiss your bride," the pastor said, snapping them both out of their trances.

Derek took Taryn into his arms and dipped her in a passionate kiss. Everyone in the crowd stood up applauding as they blew bubbles at the newlyweds.

"Yay, Mommy, Daddy!" Caylin exclaimed as she hopped off Noah's lap and ran up to her parents.

Derek picked her up and tossed her in the air before resting her on his hip with one arm. Taking his other, he wrapped it around Taryn's waist with a huge smile. They were officially a family. They had gotten their happily ever after at last.

Ten years later

Derek was still acting, but now as their two kids, Caylin and Christian, were older, he and Taryn agreed it was okay for him to go away for a few months each year to film if he got offered really good roles. But Derek always made sure to only take on roles during the school year so he could spend breaks and summer vacation with his family.

The kids were in school now, and Taryn found ways to keep herself busy. Expanding the Bennett family business to sell real estate in Hawai'i, Derek's dad hired Taryn to run their main office. Over time, she found out she had a real talent for customer service and selling houses. Taryn was still teaching but only her online courses for the University of San Francisco.

Despite this, she was still in touch with her vice principal and coworkers at the high school and found out with recent pay cuts, many were struggling to find reasonable rent for a decent place. She and Derek decided to purchase other town homes, similar to the one they already owned, to rent out to teachers in such situations for reasonable rates if they signed contracts to stay at the school for at least five years. The rental properties eventually paid for themselves and was the best investment they could have made for their kids' futures.

"Hey, handsome," Taryn said one Saturday morning as she entered the bedroom of their new house.

"Hey, beautiful." Derek smiled back as he stretched his arms over his head in their king-size bed.

"I really love our new house, baby. All our hard work is finally paying off," Taryn said as she climbed in and curled up next to his side.

"I love it too. I thought five bedrooms was excessive, but Cay and Chris both have their own rooms, we have ours, there's a guest room for when our family comes to stay, and that office of yours can always be turned into another room for a third baby." Derek sighed happily as he wrapped his arms and legs around Taryn.

"Oh yeah?" she said teasingly.

"Uh-huh," he replied, thrusting his hip into her side. His cock was rock hard already. "Wait, where are the kids?"

"My parents came by like crazy people about twenty minutes ago to take them on a surprise trip to the zoo. They figured since you just got back yesterday from shooting in New York, we could use a day to ourselves," Taryn said, turning to face him.

She slowly dragged her hand from his chest, down his abdomen, until her fingertips were resting at the edge of the elastic on his boxers. Slipping one finger into his waistband, Taryn ran her finger from side to side between his hips as she slowly licked her lips before biting down gently on her bottom lip, pushing her front up against him on a shallow moan.

"Your parents are the best." Derek sighed as he crashed his mouth onto hers, rolling her onto her back on the bed.

Taryn's hands frantically ran across Derek's back as she maneuvered beneath him. He adjusted himself so he was resting between her thighs. She could feel her tummy muscles burn with a hungry need to have her husband inside of her again. He was only gone for a month to film this time, but it was too damn long. Slipping his hand under the seam of her pajama shorts, he ran his palm up the inside of her thighs.

"No panties?" Derek smirked as the pad of his thumb connected with her entrance.

"They were going to get in the way." Taryn panted as she shook her head. "It's been a while. Can you blame me?"

"Fuck, I've missed you." Derek groaned as he pushed his tongue past her lips.

Taryn's head dropped back with a moan as Derek moved his kisses to her neck. His fingers were making little circles at her entrance as her hands desperately pushed at the waistband of his boxers, urging him to take them off.

"Tell me what you want, baby." Derek's breathing was heavy as he tried to control his own lust for his wife.

"I want you, baby," Taryn pleaded, "inside of me."

"As you wish," Derek said, kissing her forehead before leaning back to watch her lose herself in his fingers. Slowly, he entered her with his middle finger. Her muscles clenched around him.

"Two." She panted as she gripped the bedding.

Watching her writhe under his touch, he pulled his hand back and reentered her with two fingers. Taryn's thigh muscles clenched against his sides, making him smile. Derek slowly started to pump his fingers inside of her as he took the pad of his thumb and began massaging her clit.

"Oh, Derek," she moaned as she dragged her bottom lip between her teeth. "Fuck this. I want you, baby." She panted as she reached down and gripped him through his boxers, making Derek's body jerk forward.

Suddenly, Derek was standing and kicking off his boxers at the edge off their bed. Quickly, she yanked off her shorts and top, discarding tossing them at Derek playfully. Taryn looked at him with greedy eyes as her chest heaved with desire.

"I have the most beautiful wife in the world." Derek smiled as he stood there for a second, staring at Taryn as she lay there still as breathtaking as the day they met.

"Then what are you waiting for?" She groaned.

Crawling onto the bed, he braced himself on their headboard, hovering over her. Taryn adjusted herself beneath him, her entrance hovering just beyond the length of his hardness.

"I love you, Derek." Taryn smiled as she took his face in her hands and kissed him.

"I love you too, Taryn." He sighed as he kissed her forehead.

Unable to control himself any longer, Derek's hips shot forward, his length diving into her. The familiar feel of her muscles tightening around him brought a strange comfort to his heart and sparked a fire in him that only Taryn could set. Slowly, he retreated from her depths before dipping his hips and grinding back into her, causing a moan to escape past her lips.

"I'm going to make love to you all over this house, baby," Derek teased as he continued to lose himself in his wife.

Suddenly, Derek wrapped her legs around his waist and was picking her up as he slid off the two of them off the bed, standing up, his length still hard inside of her.

"Derek, where are we going?" Taryn giggled as he walked them out of their room.

"I already told you. I'm going to make love to you everywhere, so no matter where you look when I'm away, you'll think of me," Derek said as he stopped halfway down their stairs and placed her gently on a carpeted step. "Turn around baby, brace yourself."

Listening, Taryn turned so her backside was facing him. Gripping the carpet two steps up, Taryn mentally prepared herself for his attack. Derek gently ran his hands from her shoulders, down her back, until he had one resting on each side of her bottom. His fingers dug into the tender skin as he slammed into her, causing her body to jerk forward. She could feel the entire weight of his body enter her on each advance as he used the angle of the steps to find the deepest parts of her. Taryn could feel her muscles begin to tighten as that familiar burn entered her tummy, and Derek could sense it as sounds of pleasure escaped past her lips.

"Together, baby." Derek panted.

"Oh, Derek," she moaned as her head fell backward.

"Fuck!" he shouted as their releases took them, causing him to collapse onto her back, his hips still pumping into her, milking every ounce of his essence from his body, filling her.

"I love you, Derek." She sighed, catching her breath as she felt his heartbeat thudding against her back.

"I love you, Taryn," he said, trailing a line of kisses down her spine, sending tingling shock waves across her skin. "Forever."

As they lay there on the stairs, pure bliss took over. Even after all this time, the magnetic pull that brought them together was stronger than ever, and they couldn't have been luckier to find each other. They fell in love, a love that withstood every obstacle life had thrown at them. Together, they were able to build a happy life despite the many times the world around them seemed to shatter into tiny pieces. In each other, Taryn and Derek were finally healed.

About the Author

Healed is the third and final book in the Fallen series. Recently divorced, Gianna Emiko Barnes threw herself into her writing, channeling her pain and heartbreak into it, helping to bring the experiences of the characters to life. Experiencing much loss in her life, even prior to the divorce, she learned to be resilient, staying true to herself with the endless support of her closest family and friends. As such, love, respect, and communication are three values that she lives by, helping her to embody the strength she needs to push through any and all obstacles life faces.

This series, although completely fictional, was based on multiple personal experiences she survived, emphasizing to her readers hope—that no matter what they go through as long as they stay true to themselves and their values, there will always be a rainbow at the end of the thunderstorms in life.

Although this closes the door on this series, Gianna Emiko Barnes continues to push forward with her passion of writing, hoping readers can learn from her characters' experiences and take away more from her books than a good story. She truly hopes her readers enjoyed her writing and that the Fallen series was able to give a slight escape to readers from the real world. Her first stand-alone novel is set to release in 2022, so stay tuned!

CPSIA information can be obtained
at www.ICGtesting.com
Printed in the USA
BVHW050116090822
644116BV00001B/28